FIRST SIGHT

ANNIE HOLDER

With sincere apologies to all Americans for the liberties I have taken with your language…

www.annieholder.com

HOPE

What happens if I bend forward in this? Have a little jiggle…? Nothing. Surprisingly *secure*. Too saucy for a wedding dress, though. What would my mother say if she could see me now?

I'm just glad they didn't make me do strapless. You never feel as if everything's going to stay where you put it.

EVERETT

What's the damn delay? Don't they know I'm going nuts in here? There must be a camera somewhere. I bet they're filming me sweating – keeping me here so I get my panties in a proper bunch. Better tv that way. Doesn't matter how *I* feel about it.

HOPE

I'll just see if my tummy looks bulgy…? Actually, it's encouragingly all right. Even my bum's behaving itself. Not sticking out. Not looking wobbly. Turns are there *are* some good things about two years of penury. At least you look fairly thin to marry a stranger on the telly.

Oh *God*, I'm marrying a *stranger* on the *telly*! What if he just laughs at the sight of me, mutton dressed as lamb in this hideous frock? How will I stand the mortification? I *must* stand it. That's the deal. It's what I've signed up for.

EVERETT

Jeez, I look old! I can see why they picked a grey suit, I'm so grey at the front here…and here… When did I get this way? It just crept up on me. I can't do anything about it, but what if she *hates* the way I look? What if my scar disgusts her?

HOPE

Bloody hell, what was I *thinking*? I *was* okay, and suddenly 'I'm petrified!

RACHEL DELANEY
EXECUTIVE PRODUCER 'FIRST SIGHT'

It started off with a bunch of women sitting around someone's apartment drinking wine and eating take-out, sharing maudlin stories as the evening got later and the line of empty bottles got longer.

Someone related the saga of her cousin, who'd met this guy on a dating site, it had seemed like a match made in heaven, but somehow nothing ever clicked between them. He'd finished it, telling her there was 'no spark'. She was so disappointed, and none of her friends could believe she hadn't been able to hold on to this supposedly perfect guy who'd seemed ideal for her: same demographic, same beliefs, same values, same politics. On paper, they were the perfect couple! How could it *not* work out? Someone dared to posit that it was hardly surprising, that you couldn't expect a *computer* to get it right.

The next day, I'm on the subway and it popped back into my head. It got a hold of me, and I started thinking a human being should be able to beat the algorithm every time. Stands to reason…right?

By the time I got to work, the concept of 'First Sight' was firmly embedded, and I was in the team office blurting ideas like a crazy person! One couple chosen by machine, one by humans, and another where the humans picked one subject and the machine matched their mate.

I had suits in boardrooms across town nodding sagely as we pitched the concept of the highly-watchable courtship *following* the marriage rather than preceding it. Obviously, so much wackier shit's been done since then that our little show now seems tame in comparison, but then, it was the first of its kind.

We cast the net incredibly wide thinking we'd have trouble generating interest. How wrong we were! As the trickle of applications became a torrent, we started to see what a job we'd taken on, and how it was going to be a learning curve for all of us just trying to get the thing onto the screen. It took nearly a year to get to a point where we thought we had suitable candidates…one of the hardest jobs I've undertaken in a thirty-year media career!

Nearly two years after that drunken girls' night, about to unleash my little project on the world, I was still asking the same question I'd been grappling with through my hangover on the subway that morning.

Can you engineer the thunderbolt?

PART I:

'The How'

HOPE

Popping to the pricey supermarket near work to riffle the dented tins, I saw them. I recognised him first, of course. He was a lot greyer, had grown a beard, and changed the style of his glasses.

I was standing, gawping, getting in everyone's way, when he turned to speak to his companion and I realised it was *her*: Jocasta. Crushingly, she'd already reverted to her pre-pregnancy figure, like a giraffe in leather jeggings. A willowy, glamorous, husband-nicking giraffe. She clutched reins in one hand, at the other extreme of which strained a chubby toddler, utterly absorbed in removing potatoes one by one from the display before his little nose, squatting to place them in an orderly line on the floor. He was beautiful, with lovely, chunky limbs like juicy sausages, huge blue eyes, and a shock of tousled, carroty hair sticking out in every direction from his round little head.

The sight of that mop of fire took my breath away. Justin was dark, with brown eyes and hair. Jocasta always appeared exotically foreign to me, with her olive skin and the black curls she tossed spiritedly as they bickered about what to buy. *I'm* the redhead. That lovely little boy was what *my* son should have looked like! *I* wouldn't have ignored him while I rowed over the ready-meals! I would have bought a shop's-worth of potatoes and made lines of them across the floor all day with him if that's what he wanted to do! Where had the red hair come from? It must be some quirk in the gene pool, delivering this most Pictish of babies to his Mediterranean mother.

Finally, Jocasta deigned to notice what her child was doing, and yanked sharply on the reins with a gasp of admonition. A moment's incomprehension at being tugged from his potato-piling reverie, then the inevitable crying started. It took every ounce of my self-control not to rush over and gather him up in my arms, soothing his distress. Red-faced with mortification, Jocasta seemed satisfyingly at sea. Shoving the reins at his father, who to his credit did pick him up and attempt to distract him with a bunch of keys, she bent and hastily scooped up the potatoes, dropping them carelessly into the nearest container.

I moaned in my throat as the baby wailed on. Tutting, glaring shoppers edged irritably past as I stood rooted to the spot in the centre of the aisle a maximum of eight feet from Justin and his new family. Coming to my senses abruptly, I realised I needed to get away before they saw me.

Taking a frantic step backwards, my cumbersome handbag caught and swept half a shelf of glossy periodicals across the shiny supermarket floor. Keeping my back to Justin, I rushed to scrabble them up and restack them. In my haste, I trod on one and ripped the cover half off with my high heel. Swearing under my breath, I pushed it into the basket with the rest of my spartan shopping and sprinted to the self-service checkout so I didn't have to look anyone in the eye.

At home, I curled on the bed and shovelled in a limp and browning salad without tasting it, listlessly flicking through the overpriced magazine I hadn't wanted and could ill-afford. The advertising was depressing. All the things I could once have had – and would still have been able to acquire were it not for my malfunctioning ovaries. Reading articles trumpeting the successes of other women's careers, wardrobes, interior design and sex lives sent my mood spiralling further downward to a point where I felt so sick I was unable to finish everything on my plate. Before, I'd thrown things away the moment they reached the arbitrary date printed on the label. Now, I regarded wasting food as a heinous crime, given how insufficient my weekly budget had become over my two years as a supposedly independent woman.

Tossing the magazine aside sulkily, a wadge of leaflets slid out. I glanced hopefully through them in case there were any money-off vouchers. One was a different size from the rest, on unusual paper, and decidedly American in tone and appearance. I read it all, and in that moment felt like an imprisoned princess craning out of her turret at the far horizon, sure she's just caught the distant sound of heroically-chinking armour on the benign breeze.

In a frenzy, I filled in the whole form without an instant's hesitation, and only came to my senses when I was scratching in the dresser drawer, certain I still had an airmail envelope, somewhere… Telling myself to get a sodding grip, I shoved the whole lot into the recycling basket, stood at the kitchen sink, finally opened the vodka I'd been saving for a special occasion, and drank half of it in fast, urgent gulps as if it was medicine. Horrified that the unexpected sight of Justin's new family had released the genie of feeling, I went to have a bath to distract myself. Flopped drunkenly in three inches of lukewarm water, I sobbed uncontrollably, finally lurching from the tub, kneeling dripping and shivering before the toilet, and vomiting a throat-burning combination of half-digested old lettuce and so-recently-swallowed spirit.

Shuddering with long-suppressed shock, I dried myself ineffectually, staggered the mercifully short distance from bathroom to bed, entombed my feeble body beneath the duvet, and prayed I'd die during the night of something quick and painless.

EVERETT

My shoulder had been bugging me all winter. After more sleepless nights than I could count, I stopped trying to be brave and went to the doctor. He manipulated the joint, cranking my arm back and forth until the pain was so bad I nearly punched him, before saying I might have arthritis in it, and I'd need a blood test.

I trooped down the hall with my chitty to wait in line for the nurse, feeling defeated as hell. Not even fifty and arthritic already? There was a long line in front of me, so I picked up a magazine to pass the time. A leaflet slid out onto the floor. I retrieved it, glanced, read, inwardly scoffed, and put it back on top of the pile of magazines when the nurse called my name.

I answered her questions, sat quiet and biddable in the chair like a model patient while she took my blood and filled out the paperwork, and thought of nothing else but that goddam leaflet. When she was done and I was free to go, there was only one elderly lady left in the waiting area. I realised I wanted that stupid piece of paper but I didn't want anyone to see me take it. I killed time helping myself to a cup of water from the cooler. The lady's name was called. She shuffled into the nurse's office. As soon as the door closed, I darted across, snatched up the leaflet, and shoved it in my jacket like a shoplifter in a Seven-Eleven.

I got out of there as fast as I could with shaking hands and a pounding heart, convinced someone had seen me, but what did it matter? No one else would want what I'd just picked up.

HOPE

After a formal dressing-down in front of half the office, I was forced into the dignity-shredding confession that I'd had to pay my electricity bill as a matter of urgency before they cut off my supply, and couldn't pay said debt from home because I didn't own a computer. Spotty, my embryonic superior, with a penchant for polka-dot tights and unfortunate acne to match, had simply blinked uncomprehendingly, as if I'd lapsed into Ancient Greek mid-sentence. What sort of a person didn't own a *computer*?

Forced to endure her adenoidal intonation of the paragraphs from the company handbook she considered relevant to my most recent transgression, I was eventually dismissed from her exalted presence. Seething, I marched straight from her desk into the stationery cupboard, and helped myself to an airmail envelope and the required quantity of stamps without permission.

EVERETT

"Everett, get real! Don't you think the girls who've applied are more likely to be interested in the prize money? They probably couldn't give a crap about finding Mr Right. They just wanna be on tv!"

"Whatever. It's only a maybe, anyway. I might not even get picked."

Mel won't quit, "What about those goddam forms like the White Pages?"

"I guess they're a good way to whittle out the timewasters...?"

"So, why do you have to go all the way to New York for more of the same?"

"This is my showbiz screen-test, Mel! Regardless of whether they liked what I wrote on all those forms, if I'm shit on camera, I'm coming home."

Shane poked my leg, "You said 'shit'!"

Jesse smirked. Mel rolled her eyes.

"Shhh! Tell-tale! Mom didn't notice..."

Melanie treated me to the death-stare they obviously take you aside and teach you as soon as you become a mother, "I noticed, Shane. I just chose to ignore it. I'm starting to think Uncle Everett is beyond help."

"I might get there and not look right. I might be too old, or too scruffy, or too – "

"Clinically insane?"

"Melanie Cole, don't you *want* me to be happy?"

"I do, Everett McCann! More than anything, that's what I want. That's what we *all* want. We love you and we want you to get the very best from your life. But, sugar, this ain't the way! If you'd said how you were feeling, I could have fixed you up with – "

"Oh no, Mel! I've met your friends. They're all terrifying. I just want a *normal* girl…"

"Everett, 'normal girls' do not marry strange men for money on television!"

Jesse leant back in his chair, pushed his plate away, lit a cigarette, "The other problem, of course, is she *could* be a moose…"

I round on him, "You know what, I don't even care! I don't care if she's got one leg and a lazy eye! What's so goddam great about me that I can afford to be choosy? I just want someone to smile when I walk in the door, talk to me about their day, show an interest in me – "

"Until the stipulated twelve months is up, and the one-legged, boss-eyed Mrs McCann collects her prize money and hops off into the sunset…and you'll be in a worse state than you are now, because you'll be lonely *and* heartbroken! Just let *me* fix you up with somebody. You remember Belinda? She's single. She's always liked you, Everett."

"Belinda…?"

Jesse smacked my arm, "You must remember, man! Busty Belinda? Had the 'wardrobe malfunction' at the fancy dress dance?"

"Oh, *that* Belinda! Yeah, I remember…"

Mel rolled her eyes, persevering, "Well, she's had the hots for you for years. Why don't I call her and see if she's free Friday?"

"No, Mel. Thank you, but no thank you. I have no desire to be better acquainted with Busty Belinda than I already am."

"What's wrong with her?"

"She's...she's... Oh, she's *dumb*, Mel! Her head is emptier than that prairie down there!"

"Oh!" Melanie's loyally offended on her buddy's behalf.

"Sorry... Look, I understand you don't wanna see me get my hopes up for nothing, but I need to crawl out of this rut I'm stuck in or my life is never gonna change. I'll be living like this 'til they carry me out in a box! If I don't get picked, I'll still have had a nice New York vacation, and I'll have seen behind the scenes on a tv show. Not everyone can say that! And think of the promotion for the ranch, Mel! We'd never be able to afford a slick tv campaign, but if I get on this show, we get one for free!"

Jesse nudged his wife, "Now, Mel, that is a damn practical idea."

Melanie scowled and began collecting up the dirty plates, "Well, Everett, you're obviously in full self-destruct mode and nothing I say will make any difference."

"You know what you should say?"

"What?"

"Good luck. God Speed."

"You're crazy, you know that? And *you've* been no help!" She rounded aggressively on her husband, who held up his palms in a gesture of surrender, "Hey, don't you involve me in this! You know you're wastin' your breath. He's always been demented and he ain't gonna change now. He's a big boy, honey. He's made his choice, let him do his thang."

HOPE

When one of the show's producers rang my mobile at 3.00pm on a dreary Tuesday, I thought it was a nuisance call and nearly rejected it. It took a moment to realise it was a New York number! Snatching up my phone, I left the switchboard ringing off the hook and charged into the stationery cupboard.

A chatty woman called Rachel informed me, with typical American pizzazz, that I was down to the last four in my age group, my presence was required in New York for final selection, and I was provisionally top of their list! After absorbing this marvellous bombshell with as much composure as I could muster, scribbling down the details with a handy nearby pad and pen, I did a secret, silent, high-kicking conga up and down the cramped cupboard, wiped the smile off my face with difficulty, reopened the door and almost walked slap-bang into Spotty, who'd clearly been listening outside. She stood before me with one eyebrow raised. I noted the company bible clamped under her arm like a nervous swimmer clutches a float.

I smiled expansively, carefully closed the cupboard door, steered a circuitous path around her, and walked unhurriedly back to the Reception desk. Eight incoming lines buzzed with insistent electronic urgency from the switchboard, red lights flashing. Spotty flicked to a particularly well-thumbed section of the handbook and began spouting corporate policy on receiving personal calls during work time, and abandoning a post outside of a designated break.

Still smiling broadly, I let the 'phones ring on, put on my coat, and swung my handbag over my shoulder. Her officious, plummy voice died in her throat as I cheerily explained I'd been 'headhunted for a US media role' and must leave for New York within the week. After a second or two of absolute silence – apart from the trilling telephones – she burbled some vindictive pettiness about working my full notice if I expected to get paid. With breezy unconcern, I took great delight in informing her that my paltry wages were of no consequence, my new salary was six figures, and I would greatly appreciate her posting on my P45 with appropriate urgency.

Halfway to the main door, I caved in to temptation, turned smartly on my heel, and strolled jauntily back to her frozen figure. Leaning forward, I placed my hand on her arm and advised condescendingly, "A little tip for the future, when you're a big, grown-up girl. I'd stop matching my tights to my complexion if I were you. As you talk out of your arse most of the time, it makes it almost impossible to determine which way up you are."

I left her staring after me, mouth opening and closing like a dying turbot. Free of my veneer and glass prison, I ran all the way to the tube station like a kid on the first day of the holidays.

EVERETT

New York was the noisiest, smelliest, rudest place I'd ever been. Have you seen that movie *Crocodile Dundee*, where he tries to stroll down the sidewalk to take the place in, but is powerless against the tide? That's how I felt. I got sick of being jostled. At first I'd apologise, but I soon gave that up because no one reacted or even broke their stride. The wall of ceaseless noise; the sea of hard, unemotional faces: in the end, I mostly stuck to the hotel. At least it was quiet in there, and I could pound the gym when I felt cooped-up. Out in the street, I couldn't hear myself think.

There were twelve of us guys, four in each age group. Some of them were chatty, but most treated the communal evening meals (filmed, naturally) as a chance to score points off everyone else. I didn't think that was the way to go about it. I figured if you just behaved how you always would – no bullshit, no machismo – then they could see how you'd be through a lens. If you lacked the spark they were searching for they wouldn't pick you, no matter how many smart shots you landed at your rivals' expense.

I tried to extract as much from the experience as I could, if only to recount it to Shane when I got home, but I wasn't disappointed to leave the city. I didn't know whether I'd be chosen. I couldn't get a feel for what they thought of me. The other guys were younger, more sophisticated, and all college-educated like my brother, Ralton. I was certainly the odd man out. It had previously made me notable, but tv shows are aspirational and who'd aspire to be me, a worn-out old cowboy who just wanted someone to share his quiet little life?

Members of the 'FIRST SIGHT' Production Team:
RACHEL DELANEY – Executive Producer
DIANA MAURICE – Programme Consultant
VASQUEZ HERNANDEZ – Series Editor

<u>Hope Howarth</u>

Rachel: Hope was a cold fish. She made it hard to choose her. I really *wanted* her on the show because she was so different, but she was also so closed off, so formal, so…so…

Vasquez: British!

Rachel: Right! It's a stereotype, but she was prim, proper, serious, watchful, kinda sarcastic…she came over as a bitch! But on her forms, she'd been this sweet, vulnerable individual crying out for someone to notice her. She had *edge*…but she refused to show it.

Vasquez: Rachel wanted to have Hope so much, but she was bumming every screen test she did…so in the end I took her aside and told her she was going home unless she loosened the fuck up. I've never seen anyone look so indignant and so crushed at the same time.

Rachel: I mean, it worked though, huh? From the moment we received her forms, I just got this impression she was hanging by a thread. After Vasquez's 'bad cop' routine, it was almost as if she decided, 'Fine. Have it your goddam way. But if I'm going out, I'm going out like me.'

Everett McCann

Diana: Oh. My. God.

Rachel: Vasq, you can't speak to this, but all the girls on the team were head over heels in love with Everett.

Vasquez: And he was the wild-card pick!

Rachel: Yeah, he was! The other three suggested themselves early on as good, safe bets, and then Everett's application came in quite late.

Diana: It was *so* different, he was too intriguing to ignore.

Rachel: Sure, and when we met him…!

Vasquez: Oh, they were *all* pathetic about Everett. Just because he had an accent and said 'Ma'am' and opened doors and stood up when they came in, and…oh, he just made all the rest of us look bad! He seemed *such* a caricature that I think it got under the other guy's skins a little.

Diana: Yeah, it appeared so artless, that whole 'homespun charm' thing…and yet every time I interviewed him I was left with this impression that he actually knew *exactly* what he was doing. He was just too interesting a character to pass over.

Vasquez: I personally went into it thinking the twenty-somethings – the 'computer match-up' – would be the most watchable pairing, but it was the two bruised oldies just looking for a port in life's storm who ended up delivering the tv gold.

EVERETT

The nice Celebrant whips us through our vows in record time while I try not to fluff my lines or sound too much like a dumb hick.

Before I can get my head around what's happening, I'm a married man, and my new wife and I are shunted into an adjoining room while the cameras turn to capture the second ceremony of this extraordinary day.

We're left alone, facing one another in the middle of a small lounge with a fixed camera in one corner. Not touching, not talking, just standing and staring.

My wife's name is Hope. The significance of that isn't lost on me. She has a soft, clear voice and an English accent. She has flame-red hair pulled into a thick bun on the side of her head, secured with a ring of flowers. Her skin is pale, and there's a dusting of freckles across her nose and cheeks. Her eyes are very green and bright, and her smile is wide and infectious. When she beams up at me, I can't help but grin back like an idiot.

Her dress is cream lace, and it shows off every curve. I try to avoid being a typically-oafish guy just gawping at her body. To take my mind off the contents of Mrs McCann's wedding gown, I try to picture Jesse and Mel's faces when I introduce her. Not a lazy eye or a wooden leg in sight! I'm troubled by the sudden notion it's all too good to be true. What's the downside? My shaky self-confidence stutters when I consider the downside might be me.

I can't think of anything intelligent to say. I just gaze at her, and try to figure out what she makes of me.

"Is it two 'n's?"

"Huh?"

"McCann. Two 'n's?"

"Yeah."

"Okay." She nods once, decisively. Get the admin done first. I guess it *is* important to know how to spell your own name.

She looks at the floor for a moment, as if plucking up courage, and then asks quietly, "How did you get that big scar?"

I knew it. She hates the way I look. Goddam Martin Parker! The man's been dead for thirty years and he's still screwing things up for me!

I whisper, "Do you hate it?"

Concern fills her bright eyes. She takes a tentative step forward and places skinny fingers on my forearm, "No, it's not that! It's… I just wondered how, that's all…"

I like that she's trying to spare my feelings. I tease, "How do you *think* I got it?"

Poker-faced. "Duelling? Lion taming? Very, *very* undercooked shark sandwich?"

She's funny. I'm chuckling even as I weigh up whether to tell the whole truth. "It's not as much fun as any of those."

"What happened to you?"

"My Mom's boyfriend cut me with a broken bottle."

"Bloody hell! How old were you?"

"Seventeen."

"Why'd he do it?"

I hesitate momentarily. "Um…he was trying to hurt my Mom and I was trying to stop him. I put him on his ass and he didn't like that, so he came at me with a broken bottle and sliced my face open."

Eyes round as saucers, mouth a perfect pout of astonishment, "You could have lost an eye!"

"I guess I was lucky, then."

"Is he still on the scene?"

"No. He…died."

"Couldn't have happened to a nicer bloke. What about your Mum?"

Mentioning Mom always stings, deep inside. I manage, "She's dead too."

She doesn't spout empty platitudes about being sorry over people she's never met, and I like that about her. She nods thoughtfully, asking, "Is your Dad still alive?"

"Dunno. Never met the guy."

She slaps one little white hand over her eyes, "It's the put-your-foot-in-it Olympics here, isn't it? As you can see, I'm a gold medal contender!"

I grin. "My family's a bit of a hornet's nest. Poke around and a whole swarm of trouble flies out. You weren't to know."

"Is there *anything* good about them?"

"Sure there is! I've got a little brother. I'm very close to him. He's doing real good for himself. He's more than a brother, really. He's the son I never had."

"A nice look comes on your face when you talk about him."

"I love him."

"I can see that." She's watching me very intently. I wonder why she's here, going through with this crazy stunt.

"Is your family as much of a train-wreck as mine?"

"Less so, by the sound of it. My Dad left when I was twelve – couldn't take the rowing any more. They got divorced and he went to work abroad. He sends the odd Christmas card. Some years he remembers, anyway..." A regretful smile crosses her face, "He's not senile or anything, he's just not that bothered about being a Dad...so I'm not that bothered about being a daughter in retaliation. Petty, really."

"How about your Mom?"

"She's a formidable character! Single Mums are, aren't they? I do love her and everything, but she frustrates me because she always sticks her oar in. I *think* it's because she wants the best for me…?"

"I'm sure it is."

"She just has a lot of opinions – quite vocal ones – about the life-choices I make."

"She must have been off the chart about this!"

"…I haven't told her."

"Wanna hear something funny?"

"What?"

"I haven't told my brother either!"

She throws her head back and laughs unselfconsciously.

"I was just going to rock up on his doorstep with you: 'Surrrpriiise!'"

She's giggling, "That sounds quite fun… Good telly!"

"Gotta keep the ratings up! Could be our Honeymoon, huh." I ponder how nice it would be to curl up somewhere cosy and quiet with Mrs Hope McCann, slide her luscious-looking body free of the cream lace…

The door opens behind me and makes me jump. I feel the heat of a blush on my cheeks and neck.

It's Rachel from the production team, "Press call! Photos, a few questions from journos, coupla pieces to camera. You ready?"

I look down at my new wife, offer her my arm. She slides her delicate fingers around it and holds on tight as we follow Rachel back out into the harsh glare of the lights.

PART II:

'The Why'

EVERETT

When I think as far back as I can remember, every early memory is coloured golden by the smoky tinge of dusty, desert light. The sun eternally shone. There were hordes of fascinating people to talk to, laughter was frequent and unselfconscious, and a campfire always burned long into a starlit night. I don't think an evening went by when I didn't fall asleep to the hypnotic crackle and pop of the flames, the low murmur of voices, the whisper of warm wind in the trees.

Of course, I didn't know then that other people lived in houses and not in tents, trucks, or under the stars. I didn't know that other people had Daddies who owned cars they drove from their houses to their jobs and back, day after day in the same place, seeing the same people. I thought everybody drifted. The smells of pot and campfire are the evocative scents of my childhood. There were always so many people around because no one had a job, and they were all perpetually smiling because everybody was stoned.

I *had* a Daddy, obviously. He just didn't stick around. Life was like that. Relationships were transient, homes impermanent, faces came and went. I was at Woodstock, but I don't remember it. I know I was there because I have a dog-eared photograph. A fat, naked baby nestled on his mother's lap on the grass in a huge crowd that stretches back across the hillside as far as you can see. My mother has brown hair past her waist, a long dress, and butterflies painted on her cheeks. She's laughing, and so am I. There's a man sitting next to her, close to her, and that's my Daddy, or so my Mom always said. He's turned away from the camera so you can't see his face, but he's wearing old jeans, a red shirt, and a battered, wide-brimmed hat with feathers around it like some Indian chief. He's got long, blonde hair hanging down underneath the hat, the soles of his bare feet are filthy, and one tanned hand holds my tiny fist in it…and all I know of him is the back of his head.

I used to look out for him everywhere we went. All I had to go on was a hat and a bad haircut, but still I stared hopefully at every likely-looking guy who passed us in the street, just in case one of those fellas was my long-gone Pop.

HOPE

It's a flash in the pan! Jocasta: is that even actually a *name*? Sounds like a variety of bedding plant to me! He'll get over it. Nearly twenty years and we're in a big rut, that's all. He's got a bit bored and let some silly little girl turn his head. All the tests say there's nothing wrong with me, and it's not as if I'm so old that it's a lost cause. Telling me he'd 'waited quite long enough' – like there's some sort of time limit on a barren marriage. As if it's solely my fault, my responsibility! All this Jocasta-crap is a stupid mid-life ego massage. He'll get it off his chest and come crawling back. We'll laugh about this in six months' time!

EVERETT

I call him Parker because the guy doesn't deserve a Christian name. Hell, he doesn't deserve me wasting good oxygen on him, but I can't explain all of this properly without talking about Parker.

Without Parker, there wouldn't be Ralton, so Parker's the reason I never had the chance of a meaningful relationship of my own. Parker's the reason I ended up in a shiny suit in a New York hotel thinking 'bout the stupidest thing I'd ever done in all my stupid life was sign myself up to marry a stranger.

Parker was a Vietnam vet. He was also flat-out crazy. He smoked a lot of weed, which just increased his paranoia. Whenever a helicopter went over the trailer park, Parker'd shake like a leaf and make everybody get under the table. As he spiralled deeper into his own personal hell, it became ever more apparent he was dragging my Mom down with him. By the time she discovered she was pregnant again, all the fight had pretty much left her.

HOPE

Every time the 'phone rings I think it's him, but it turns out to be yet another of my mother's friends organising a get-together. Since when did *her* life get so chock-full of fun? My friends don't ring – probably because I don't have any. What I *had* were the wives of Justin's mates, and that parks them all firmly on his side, not mine. In fact, without my husband, I don't seem to have anything at all. I certainly don't have the energetic, stimulating life of my retired mother. Anyone would think I was *jealous* of her!

When I was twelve, the Dad I adored got offered a posting in Zurich. He elected to take the job, but not his family. I couldn't understand why we didn't go too. I decided it had to be something to do with my mother and the way she treated him: cutting, critical, witheringly sarcastic.

I suppose it *was* better once he left. My mother's shoulders dropped from around her ears and she stopped snapping at everything I said or did. She redecorated our bedrooms and smiled at me a lot more. Day to day, I didn't notice Dad's absence too much. Largely disengaged from family life, he treated parenting like a hobby he could happily set aside at will.

Initially, Dad sent me postcards from Switzerland. I'd show Mum, and she'd roll her eyes and caution me not to expect too much. I didn't know what she meant by that. The first birthday he was away, I got a fifty-pound note in my card! Mum held it up to the light to check it was real. After a few months, the postcards stopped. I wondered how Mum had known they would. I didn't tell her, because I didn't want her to know she'd been right. We barely talked about Dad after that. Mum never mentioned him, and the longer he was gone, the more courage I needed to bring up the subject.

She wasn't anti-men, but she believed in self-reliance, dignity and pride. She didn't want me to marry Justin. She thought I was too young. She wanted me to complete my degree and begin a career. I didn't care to listen. I thought she was just a bitter divorcee. Anyway, I wouldn't *need* a degree! Justin had it all worked out. He planned everything. Five years for him to make partner, and then we'd start our family. He made it sound so effortless it was impossible not to agree. I *always* agreed with Justin.

He certainly fulfilled his side of the bargain, hitting every specified mark with the precision of a prima ballerina. Humiliatingly, I clod-hopped around in the background on my two left feet, and ruined the whole show.

EVERETT

I liked my half-brother, Ralton. I used to hold him on my lap and he felt much more solid and strong than I thought a baby would. He'd wave his little arms and legs in the air, and grip my finger real tight in his fist. It made me think of that picture of my Daddy at Woodstock, holding my tiny hand in his big one.

Parker kinda liked Ralton too, but only when he was asleep. When he woke up and cried, Parker would threaten my mother with all kinds of hell if she didn't shut him up. Sometimes, if we didn't get to Ralton quickly enough, Parker would pick him up and shake him like a ragdoll, which only made him cry the louder. If I could, I'd race to the bassinet and snatch him up, hold him to my chest and curl my body around him while Parker kicked me instead, in the ribs and back and legs with his big, heavy boots, as if he could transfer his own pain if he hoofed you hard enough.

Even back then, I somehow realised he didn't have to like me – I was another man's child – but I never understood how he could hurt Ralton.

Before Parker, it had been Mom and I against the world. Now, she was on a raft and I was on the shore. She was floating away and I couldn't get her back. Increasingly, I cared for Ralton because there was no one else to do it. Parker was out God only knew where, and Mom just lay on the bed, stared at the ceiling, and didn't talk, or blink, or move.

I'd put baby Ralton in the papoose, take a bottle of formula and some slices of bread, and go exploring. Ralton didn't mind. He seemed to like it. When he was tiny, he'd just sleep as I tramped off somewhere – anywhere that wasn't the trailer – and only wake up when he was hungry or his diaper was full. As he got older, he'd grip his fat little fists in my hair and squeak in excitement at everything we saw: a bird, a fox, a cat, a cow.

Across the back of the trailer park was the rear of a big, sprawling ranch. We used to go over and pet the horses grazing in the closest paddock. I loved their calmness, the quiet reassurance of standing amongst the huge, warm bodies as if I was a part of the herd. Ralton used to reach out his baby fingers, and the horses would sniff at us with their massive, flaring nostrils, and push their soft, hot noses against our palms.

I noticed there was a blackboard up outside the gate, saying Stable Hand Wanted. I went inside, explained with imperturbable fluency that I should be given the job despite my few years and diminutive stature because our mother was sick, and I needed to earn money to buy formula for my baby brother. I stated my case with total confidence because I didn't know children weren't supposed to have jobs, and whatever I said did the trick. Unbelievably, they took me on. At the age of twelve I began working with horses, and they've been the backbone of my career ever since. You know where you are with animals. Their needs are simple, their intelligence instinctive, and their trust, once earned, is yours forever. They can read you on a fundamental level, detect the basic goodness in your soul, and they will nurture you if you're broken.

There was a solidarity about standing in the centre of that crush of shifting, snorting, steaming bodies; a sense of moving with ancient rhythms defined and understood by every living thing, transcending the meaningless boundaries of language and species. I knew true peace for the first time since Parker came into our lives, and I enjoyed doing something where I could see the direct results of my labours. If I shovelled manure all day, my buddies the horses were comfortable on fresh, sweet-smelling straw. If I groomed horse after horse, they enjoyed the attention, it kept them healthy, and cemented the bond I had with each individual creature on that ranch. I knew all their names, they'd come to me when I called them, and I'd brush them 'til they shone.

Ralton thrived in the gentleness of the environment. He'd sleep on my back in the papoose while I mucked out, and when he woke up, I'd give him his formula and talk to him, and he'd listen and watch me unblinkingly with his big, brown eyes. As he grew, he'd toddle around the stable as I worked, sticking his hands in the cold-water trough and pushing the broom, trying to copy me as I swept. On my breaks, we'd sit on the porch with the rancher's gentle wife, and draw numbers and letters on scrap paper, or read children's books from the Library. After lunch, Ralton and I would go back to the stables. We'd brush the horses together, sing songs, and listen to the birds calling and the wind rushing in the trees, making a sound like falling rain despite the dry desert air. I collected all my wages, hid them in a tin under the trailer, and waited for the day when Mom would get better and I could afford three bus tickets for her, Ralton and I to get the hell away from goddam Martin Parker.

****

Years passed.

As Parker's infantry-honed body got fatter, slower and more screwed-up, so his absolute power over us all waned a little. He still terrorised, shouted, threatened and punched, but either he was getting weaker or we were coping better. And all the while I was growing up. Five years spent at hard physical toil in all weathers toughened me. Puberty hit, passed, and the reedy, malnourished, battered little kid with a baby on his back became a broad, strong, fit young man of six feet four at seventeen.

My mother noticed this, and rallied. Some of the shadow of defeat left her. She started to wash her hair again, wear clean clothes and leave the trailer. She was even persuaded to come to the ranch with us, sit in the sun outside the stable, pet the horses and watch me work. She was beginning to see what I could not; that if I chose, I could easily flatten Martin Parker with one punch. I'd spent eight years being pushed around by him and was conditioned to view him as my aggressor. It never crossed my mind I'd grown into more than a match for him.

HOPE

I waited. I was nothing if not patient. In one way or another, I'd been waiting for nineteen years. Whenever the doorbell rang, I'd rush to answer it. It would be the postman, milkman, man to read the meter. Never Justin pledging undying love in the rain/snow/falling blossom like a scene from a Richard Curtis film. Like a teenage girl waiting impatiently for a boy to call, I'd beat my mother to the 'phone every time it rang, only to have to sheepishly surrender the receiver into her outstretched hand. When the divorce papers arrived, no one was remotely surprised but me.

EVERETT

It started as a day like any other. As I got Ralton washed and dressed in the early-morning light, tiptoeing and whispering as we always did, who should accost me at the door but my unusually bright-eyed mother, looking more alert and like her old self than she had in years. She whispered that we should talk, later, when I got home from work and Parker was invariably at the roadhouse. That evening, as we ate, my Mom outlined her intention to escape from Parker once she'd scraped together enough cash to do it. I told her about the tin, the money I'd saved, my dream of the bus tickets. Deciding there was no time like the present, as we were packing and excitedly considering where we might go, who should waltz in upon the happy planning but Martin Parker himself, drunk, wasted, and crazy with rage.

Parker went for my Mom in a way I'd never seen, tearing at her clothes, gripping fistfuls of her hair, pushing his big, bloated body onto hers, pinning her against the refrigerator. At first, paralysed with revulsion, I just stood and stared, trying to put myself between the appalling scene and the petrified Ralton. Instead of submitting and letting it happen as she commonly would, Mom begged me to save her.

Whatever was holding me back – that instinctive fear of Parker – crumbled in the face of such a direct plea for help from my beloved mother. I charged up to them and ripped the body of Parker away from my Mom with an ease that stunned me. I hadn't been aware of my latent strength. I effortlessly threw Parker to the floor and turned to reach protectively for Mom, who was already backing across the kitchen towards the cowering Ralton.

Startled by a sudden sound of shattering glass behind me, I turned, just in time to see Parker lurching to his feet wielding the stub of a beer bottle. Caught off-guard as he swung it towards me, I was unable to avoid the jagged shard that sliced my face from upper lip to cheekbone. The instant, searing pain was worse than anything he'd ever inflicted, and I yelled at the shock of it, staggering backwards and thudding down the kitchen units to slump onto the floor, half-insensible, blood already pumping. Snarling, Parker advanced on me with the broken bottle. I truly think he intended to cut my throat, but he never got the chance. To my surprise – and his, judging by the look on his face – my mother rammed the largest kitchen knife we had straight into Parker's right-hand side as he raised his arm to finish me. It went in his waist up to the plastic hilt, and protruded at least an inch out front.

For a moment, there was no sound and no movement, as Parker first looked at the knife tip sticking through his black t-shirt, then rolled incredulous eyes towards my mother. Then he started to scream, high-pitched like a little girl, pulling at the tip of the knife as if that would extract it, slicing his fingertips to ribbons on the razor-sharp point. Hauling Ralton from underneath the table by his wrists and pushing him towards the door, my mother rushed to me and dragged me past the writhing, squealing figure of Parker on the kitchen floor. The blood from his wound was spreading in thick, red streaks across the dirty linoleum as she tugged me over his kicking feet and bodily out into the dust, crying for someone to get an ambulance, crushing my bleeding head against her chest, rocking, sobbing and telling me she was sorry again and again, as if only her abject prostration and grief could keep me from dying in the dirt.

HOPE

I locked myself in my room like a child and refused to come out. After two days, my mother got her neighbour, a burly Polish scaffolder called Pawel, to come round and shoulder the bedroom door down.

Pawel brushed bits of disintegrated door frame off his t-shirt, nodded formally to me, received the embarrassed thanks of my mother with a pained expression, and went back to No. 23 without a word.

My mother and I just stood there staring at each other, until I started crying. Once I began, I found I couldn't stop. To my amazement, my mother never said 'I told you so', but crossed the room and put her arms around me in a way she hadn't since before my father left and my suspicion and mistrust drove a wedge between us. I cried for a long time, but you get to the point where you're all cried out. I felt like a deflated lilo, shoved in the loft until next summer. Everything in my life had been about Justin. He'd made every plan, every decision, earned every penny and selected how we spent it. I'd just been a passenger. It appeared the time had finally come to pilot my own craft, and I was afraid to do it.

EVERETT

Once they'd stitched me up, you could see it wasn't as bad as everyone had first thought. Ralton said I looked like Freddy Krueger and that it was 'cool'. All I knew was it hurt like hell and I didn't recognise myself when I looked in the mirror.

Free of the hospital, I wanted to return to the trailer, but the childcare lady who'd been assigned our case explained we couldn't go back there. It was late, so we were put in a Motel for the night. I soothed a fractious Ralton to sleep, then tiptoed out of our room and across to Veronica's. We were twenty-one-year-old Veronica's first post-qualification case, and she was undeniably more shaken by the whole experience than either of us. With just the right balance of firmness and flirtation, I wangled from the trembling young woman the information that Parker was incontrovertibly dead, having bled out on the kitchen floor while my mother knelt and wailed hysterically in the trailer park dirt, and various neighbours attempted to comfort Ralton and staunch my bleeding until the ambulance arrived. She then had a good old cry about the shock of it all, while I held her tight, stroked her hair, inhaled her perfume, and returned reluctantly to Ralton before my raging adolescent hormones caused more trouble than we were probably already in. I made sure I didn't let go of her completely until she revealed Ralton and I were required to make a police statement the next morning, and not before obtaining her heartfelt assurance that she'd pull every string possible to ensure we saw our mother while we were there.

I realised she clung to me very persistently, pressed her body incredibly close to mine, rubbed her palms across my chest, and squeezed my bicep muscles with her small hands. Confused, frightened and sore as I was, I also discovered I felt powerful, and more grown-up than I ever had. My mother had begged something of me and I had come through for her when it mattered. I recalled how easy it had been to grip hold of Parker and pull him away, the same way he'd thrown me around as a little kid. Was I stronger than I realised, or was Parker weak? Suddenly, it hit me: Parker wasn't just weak, he was dead, and Mom was in serious trouble! How could I explain to Ralton that his mother had killed his father to save his brother? Was that too confusing for a seven-year-old to take in? Maybe for a normal seven-year-old, who lived the kind of life reserved for the Veronicas of this world, but Ralton had seen things no kid should ever have to witness. Besides, I had no choice. I *had* to tell him. Every word that came out of both our mouths had to exonerate Mom.

I touched my undamaged cheek to Veronica's, thanked her for her candour, gave her the kind of lingering squeeze that would keep me awake and restless with adolescent arousal for an hour or two, and went back to Ralton.

****

Eventually, I slept, fitfully, but he woke early and cried when he remembered everything. I got him up, ran a hot bath almost to the top of the tub, dumped him in it, and eyeballed him over the pink plastic rim, having a serious man-to-man about what had happened and how we needed to help Mom. Desperate to do the right thing, he nodded earnestly and promised me he'd be brave. I scooped him out of the tub, swaddled him in a towel, and got into the still-warm water, trying to wash the rest of the encrusted blood off myself without disturbing my stitches. My face throbbed with the heat.

****

Scrubbed and combed like altar boys, we met Veronica in the diner across the street for breakfast. I noticed she blushed every time she glanced at me, and wouldn't look me in the eye. Ralton ate his own bodyweight in pancakes and told Veronica everything he knew about volcanoes, dinosaurs and space. It probably bored her rigid, but she was too kind to say so, and I was grateful to her for that. It gave me time to think, eating my eggs and bacon and staring out at the street, watching busy people going about their normal business, living their straightforward lives.

I asked Veronica for a quarter, went to the 'phone booth in back and rang Ray, my boss on the ranch. I explained what had happened, and that we had to make a statement to the cops so I couldn't come to work. There was silence on the line for so long I thought he'd gone. Eventually, he spoke, and his voice sounded as if he might be crying just a little. He said I should take as long as I needed, and if I required someone to vouch for me, he would do so without hesitation. I felt a lump of emotion in my throat, and the welling of unexpected tears in my eyes. I wasn't usually a crier. There was normally no point. I thanked Ray profusely, and hung up before I bawled down the 'phone like a baby. I went to the bathroom to buy time to pull myself together, and returned to the bashful Veronica and the sugar-filled Ralton.

I told Ralton to shut up and finish his pancakes before he put Veronica into a science coma, and winked at her across the table. She nearly tipped her coffee down her front. Previously, girls had just rolled their eyes and turned away when I tried to talk to them, but just recently I'd noticed they were a lot keener to get acquainted. I wondered how I could leverage my evident influence over the hapless Veronica to better help Mom.

****

We were shown into an interview room one-by-one, with Veronica sitting in because we were legally minors. I went first. I laid it on thick about the years of terror at Parker's hands. I reiterated Mom's desire to protect us, and that Parker had been about to cut my throat with the broken bottle. I made sure to mention Vietnam, about Parker being a trained soldier, and that he definitely knew how to kill. The cop wrote it all down, and took photographs of my stitched and swollen face. Then it was Ralton's turn. I know he made sure to say that his Daddy had been going to kill me, and he would have succeeded if Mommy hadn't stopped him, like we'd rehearsed over the edge of the tub that morning. I know, because Veronica told me in bed later on, but I'm jumping ahead...

Once we'd done our official duty, we were allowed twenty minutes with Mom. A severe lady cop sat in the corner and watched it all, and Veronica waited outside. For the first few moments, Mom just hugged us both, silent tears tracking her grubby cheeks. Then she made an effort to brighten. She examined my cut, and declared I would look very macho with a scar. Ralton sat on her lap and told her all about the Motel, the pancakes, and the new clothes Veronica had bought us from Wal-Mart on her credit card, while the lady cop's eyes widened, and I inwardly winced at the knuckle-rapping doubtless awaiting kind-hearted, easily-led Veronica when she finally got back to her office.

When it was time to go, Mom hugged us again, very hard, pressed her cheek against mine and hissed into my ear, "Take the money in that tin, take Ralton, and get the hell out of the state. It doesn't matter where you go. If you stay here, they will separate you. Get away, *tonight*. Protect your brother. Promise me."

What could I say? I whispered my fervent promise. She kissed us both repeatedly, told us how much she loved us, and how sorry she was that it had come to this. Ralton started crying, despite promising me he wouldn't, so I picked him up and he wrapped his skinny little arms and legs around me, buried his face in my neck, and put snot on my new sweater. I held my Mom's hand and looked at her as hard as I could until the lady cop said time was up. They took Mom back to the cells and Ralton and I back to Veronica. I tried to imprint that image of Mom in my head, in case it was a while until we saw her again.

Veronica explained she had to call around to find places for us to go. I looked right into her eyes and begged for one more night in the Motel. She agreed, of course. I had her right where I wanted her. Once Ralton was asleep, I put Mom's instructions into action. I tiptoed back next door and lost my virginity in urgent, fumbling, physical style to the luscious Veronica, left her snoozing, fished Ralton out of bed, dressed him on my lap, and made a run for it with my half-asleep little brother clinging to my back.

I had to return to the trailer for our money, and I needed a bag, some clothes, food…but I wasn't sure if there would be cops, so I went to the ranch, to Ray, the closest thing I'd ever had to a father. While his wife Renee settled Ralton to sleep on their couch, I explained the situation. Ray agreed to check out the lie of the land. We went down to the rear of the lot and Ray climbed the fence with an agility belying his advancing years. An agonising ten minutes passed before he returned to me, squatting anxiously in the long grass and starting at every sound. No cops, just a lot of police tape across the door. I didn't care about that. I wasn't going in the front. The bathroom window didn't shut properly, so I forced that open with little effort and cleaned out everything of use, filling bags and dropping them out of the window to Ray. Climbing out, I wriggled under the trailer to my secret hiding place, retrieved the stuffed tin of cash, and returned to the farm. I didn't mention the large pool of Parker's dried, dark blood in the centre of the kitchen floor, illuminated in the circle of torchlight, nor the fact I'd made sure to pick up a photograph of my mother and Ralton for him to keep, and that precious picture of Woodstock my Mom kept secretly in her bedside drawer.

Back at the ranch, the dawn was approaching, a halo of pink expanding on the horizon. I woke Ralton, and Renee fed us until I thought we'd pop. Ray took me out to one of the barns and wordlessly handed me the keys to a rusting RV partially covered by a tarpaulin, "She leaks a bit in heavy weather, but she goes…and it'll be security of a sort for you, boy."

I hugged Ray 'bout hard enough to crack his ribs. I wasn't the greatest driver, but I had my licence, and I'd learn. Ray had just given us a means of escape and a ready-made home rolled into one.

I went into the stable and trooped from stall to stall bidding farewell to every horse. Saying goodbye to Ray and Renee, for what I was starting to understand would be forever, was the hardest thing of all. By the time the sun began its sizzling climb up the morning sky, Ralton and I were rattling out of Arizona and into Utah. If I'd known I'd never see my mother again, I might not have left so readily.

HOPE

I expected to get half of everything, particularly when I cited Justin's adultery on the paperwork. The jilted wife *always* gets half. *Everyone* knows that. I was horrified when my solicitor informed me I was mistaken. I had made no financial contribution to the marriage whatsoever. My husband had completely supported me in every way for nineteen years. It appeared I was entitled to a minute settlement, and Justin craftily offered extra in the form of shares in his company. In the eyes of the court, he doubtless seemed more than generous. When I refused, you could see them silently labelling me difficult and ungrateful. Small wonder he wanted shot of me! Perhaps I should have accepted the shares, but I couldn't bear the idea of my prosperity remaining dependent upon his, and therefore Jocasta's too. She was still on the scene, and to add insult to injury, now hugely pregnant and velcroed to his side at every hearing. The only weapon I had left against them was vacillation. They apparently wanted to marry before the baby was born, so I dragged the process out to confound their plans. What a spiteful cow I was becoming.

Ashamed of the person the divorce was turning me into, all the fight finally left me. Delaying wouldn't make Justin want me again. Accepting the pittance that was my legal entitlement, I chalked the hard lessons down to experience, vowed never to behave so pathetically in a relationship again, and determined to start afresh. My mother, whilst being more sympathetic and supportive than I could have believed possible, nevertheless didn't suffer fools or malingerers. In Mum's opinion, I was a grown woman, must instantly stop bemoaning my lot, get off my backside, find a job, and secure a flat.

I'd never done a day's work in my life! I was unqualified, inexperienced, unskilled, and didn't even possess the redeeming features of youth or enthusiasm. I was, in short, unemployable. I would have to settle for whatever I could get. I ended up on the switchboard of an East London start-up, where all the so-called directors were pimply kids half my age. It was boring, frustrating, demeaning, and the pay was laughable, but it was that or a supermarket checkout, and I was too snooty for the latter.

I'd always lived in London, but city property was astronomically expensive. I knew I couldn't buy, so I'd have to rent. My salary was so insultingly minute I ended up with all I could afford, a grotty bedsit with paper-thin walls and a definite cockroach problem behind the bath panel. If I subsisted on baked beans, cup-a-soup and dented tins from the reject aisle, I could pay my exorbitant London rent, cover my tube fare, and have just about enough left over to keep the lights on. Saving to escape my hellish new existence was out of the question. Instead of attempting to plan for my future, I just stopped thinking about it. It was less petrifying that way. I sold my wedding and engagement rings, put the money in a savings account and tried to forget it was there, even though I wanted to spend it on a million lovely things to make life a bit more bearable.

The day the divorce was final, determining to view the event with positivity, I bought a bottle of cheap vodka from the off-licence by the station, intending to partake of a celebratory nip with my beans on toast. When I got home, I discovered the dribble of coke left in the fridge was bland and flat, and the idea of toasting such a pathetic excuse for a life a step too far even for my overactive imagination. Who was I trying to kid? I wasn't free. *Nothing* was bloody free any more, and that was the problem.

EVERETT

My mother received a reduced sentence in recognition of all she had suffered at the hands of Martin Parker, but the jury still convicted her.

Regardless of what you've been through, you can't go around stabbing people and letting 'em bleed out in front of your nose.

I read about Mom's sentencing in the newspaper. I was obviously too scared to go back to Arizona because of what I'd done: leaving without permission, taking Ralton, manipulating kind Veronica when all she'd done was try to help us. I felt especially guilty about that part, imagining the trouble she'd be in because of me, but I was nothing if not streetwise. I guessed I'd have to do some similarly shitty stuff to struggle Ralton and I through the next few years below the radar, so I figured I'd have to harden myself against feeling too much guilt for my more questionable actions.

Although my mother got years, incarceration for a soul once so accustomed to roaming free meant she lasted mere months before she took her own life. That was in the paper too, and I had to tell Ralton, and comfort him while he wailed through his confusion. I waited until he was asleep to do my own grieving. I cried with an uncontrollable force that alarmed me. I couldn't tell whether I was crying for Mom or for myself. I was frightened, and I was mad. I hadn't realised until that moment that Mom had been extracting a lifelong pledge from me, to raise her son because she knew she couldn't. I should have seen it coming, but I was still too immature to truly understand. I mourned in secret, cried with force and feeling until I could cry no more, and locked the hurt inside myself.

****

Ray's RV saved our lives. Yes, the damn thing leaked like a sieve and reeked of damp, but it had doors we could lock, windows we could fasten. It was our freedom and our home combined.

We moved around a lot at first. I was so paranoid about being caught that I didn't keep us in one place for more than a month at a time. Ralton loved it. It was an adventure. Looking at it through his eyes, I saw his life hadn't really changed that much, and the recent alterations had only served to improve it. He saw amazing things, went to new places, and no one hit him or shouted in his face. No wonder he was a happy little boy. He didn't miss his parents because he'd really had no relationship with either of them. Freedom from the tyranny of his father was a blessed relief and, since his birth, his poor mother had mostly been a distant, unreachable figure.

I was relieved he was all right, but I had so many other things to worry about that contentment was impossible. I missed Mom. I carried around her absence like a knot of pain in my guts. I missed Ray and Renee and working with the horses. I gradually came to realise no one was looking for us. We'd slipped through the cracks. No one was going to waste good money searching for white trash who didn't want to be found. Ralton and I were together and my final promise to Mom was intact. However, despite my frugality, I was rapidly burning through the tin of cash. With no chance of any welfare, I had to earn some money, fast. The only paid work I'd ever done was look after horses. I knew I was underage for getting a proper job, but I also realised I had to try, or embark upon a life of crime to support us. I didn't have the stomach or the nouse to be a crook, so I tramped from ranch to ranch asking for wrangler work.

****

I took a long, objective look at myself in the speckled mirror of the RV's bathroom after a week of being scrutinised and told to get lost by tough, weather-beaten men. Presentable wasn't doing the trick. I looked my age, which was no good at all, and was being too suspiciously clean-cut for the cowboys to comfortably trust. I needed to imply I was over twenty-one, and not an outsider but one of them. I let my emerging stubble grow, wore my grubbier jeans, second-hand boots instead of my sneakers, and a tighter t-shirt I'd all but grown out of as I bulged from adolescence into manhood.

Instead of minding my manners when the wife answered the door, I'd put my toe on the threshold, a lazy smile on my face, look 'em up and down in undisguised admiration of whatever might be under the housecoat, drawl I was a wrangler looking for employment, and might I have a word with their husband? It worked. I got a lot of coffee and cobbler while I waited in more kitchens than I cared to count, but the ranchers didn't want me any more when I was the Sundance Kid than when I'd been Marty McFly. Disheartened by my lack of success, frightened by what it might mean for our near future, I was floundering in indecision when I overheard two young Mexican guys talking in a gas station outside Cheyenne. I didn't have much Spanish, but I knew the word for 'horse', the word for 'work', the word for 'money'. Shameless, because I had to be, I left Ralton filling up the RV, strolled over, introduced myself, and started asking questions.

Turned out a good source of casual cash if you were skilled with horses was to latch on to the travelling circus that was the rodeo, and catch any crumbs they tossed your way. The more adaptable and hard-working you proved yourself to be, the greater the opportunities to earn, no questions asked. Officially, you didn't exist and you weren't on anyone-in-particular's payroll. Unofficially, you were the cheap, plentiful labour force of choice. The crowd got a show, it kept costs down, and everybody got paid. It was hard and sometimes dangerous, but as that pretty much summed up every one of my eighteen years on planet earth, I hauled ass into town to find out where and when the next rodeo would be, and Ralton and I got on the Interstate to track down the circus.

****

I relished rodeo. It was all the things I liked in one concentrated dose of noise and adrenalin. I got to be outdoors and feel free, work with horses and stock all day, see new places every week, chase pretty girls in tight t-shirts and even tighter jeans, make some real friends for a change, and feel the satisfyingly-thick bundle of notes shoved surreptitiously into my hand every Friday evening. I got to watch the competitors too, and I started to learn some life lessons the hippies had never taught me.

One guy, Jesse Cole, became my sort-of hero. Slight, wiry, blonde, with ice-blue eyes that bored right through you if you presumed to talk to him, he had the shiniest, newest RV on the lot, and strutted around clad head to toe in immaculate black with an appropriately twitchy-buttocked blonde glued to his side. He trained. He practised. He honed his craft and he won everything. If Jesse Cole rocked up, it was all about who'd be the best-of-the-rest, because you knew damn well he'd ace every discipline he entered. I yearned to be like Jesse Cole, especially when I found out he was only five years older than me. It wasn't only for the money and the shapely blonde, but because of the *aura* surrounding the man. People said he was arrogant, but I disagreed with that. He just *knew* he was better than the rest of them, and it wasn't down to luck. He got up earlier, ran further, bench-pressed heavier and practised more than any of his rivals. He had 'em beat before he even got in the ring.

After three years on the circuit and a lot of hard graft, I was in a position to compete on my own account – and I had one goal: to demote the world-beating Jesse Cole into second place.

HOPE

I was managing, that's all I can say; my name a cruelly-ironic joke. How could I be called Hope when I knew for certain none existed? Life remained a series of obstacles to be wearily clambered over. I did try to be upbeat. Some good had come out of the last few months. I'd been forced to take a critical look at my tattered character and properly patch its gaping rents. Encouragingly for my teetering self-esteem, my restricted diet had caused the rapid loss of the pounds I'd piled on with too much good living and not enough to do, delivering me the firm, tight figure I probably hadn't had since my twenties. I knew I shouldn't be ungrateful – I had my health, a job, a roof over my head – but I detested my miserable existence with every fibre of my being, and longed to escape from it.

EVERETT

It didn't take long to start winning, which surprised everyone but me. I knew I could do it because I'd emulated the work ethic of my hero. The prize-money was mind-blowing, more dollars in one weekend than I usually saw in a month. My instinct was still to stockpile, scrimp and save, but for the first time ever I had a proper job and a social security number. I wasn't invisible any more. I was a someone, rather than a nobody. Finally, I *belonged* somewhere. I had fans in the crowd who held up banners with my name on and asked for my autograph. Girls chased me down and slipped their numbers into my calloused palms. My fellow competitors clapped me on the back and welcomed me into the fold. All, that is, except Jesse Cole.

Jesse resented the instant challenge I presented to his mastery. I loved the showing off. I played to the crowd, became the Maverick to Jesse's Ice Man, and he hated it. He thought I was undermining him, turning the crowd against him. It wasn't intentional, but I suppose I did it nonetheless. I couldn't help it. I was desperately trying to be accepted, to make everyone love me to fill the hole I had inside. I became the renegade darling of the professional circuit. Everybody adored me, except for the one person whose approval I wanted the most.

I didn't give up on Jesse Cole, far from it. I'd try shaking hands with him at prizegiving. He never would, which only made the crowd catcall more. I'd try buying him numerous beers in the bar at the end of events. He never drank 'em. I'd even try whipping the crowd into a frenzy of appreciation for him when he won. He'd corner me in the stalls and accuse me of stealing his thunder. It might have stayed that way forever, me making constant and pathetic overtures of friendship and him rejecting every one, leaving us with nothing but a prickly rivalry that played out weekly in that circle of dust. The evident needle between us provoked genuine tension and excitement. Who were you for, Everett or Jesse? Raw talent or methodical technique? The crowds packed in. The organisers loved it. I wound up Jesse, who predictably rose to the bait, and the purse climbed up and up as the takings soared. I was playing a role, and I started to wonder if Jesse was too, seeing how the pantomime we'd unwittingly created was making every single person involved a little better off each week. Thing was, I could never have a civil conversation about how we could turn it to our even greater advantage, because the guy would blank me at every turn. That is, until Ralton fell in love with his wife.

****

Ralton didn't miss Mom exactly, not the way I did, but he instinctively craved female interaction, softness and comfort to cleave to in moments of uncertainty. There were always plenty of women trying to snare themselves the paydirt of a professional rider. Jesse Cole was spoken for, so all the action came my way instead. I enjoyed it, but couldn't exploit it the way I wanted to. Try getting amorous in a leaking RV across the gangway from a snoring kid. Trust me, it can kill even the most ardent passion. Attraction never had the chance to mellow into tenderness because I had my promise to keep to Mom. I *had* to put Ralton first. It meant all my energies had to go into earning money to support us, finance his future, and educate him the best way I could, which invariably meant educating myself too, just to keep up with the little nerd. I had no free time left for cultivating a potential wife, or even a regular girlfriend. I got my share of casual sex, but that was as far as it went. It was fun, but it was shallow.

Ralton fell in love with Jesse's wife on the very day of his thirteenth birthday. Mrs Melanie Cole was Texan, blonde, blue-eyed, honey-tanned, and her curvaceous body jiggled invitingly as she strutted her stuff around the lot, the wife of the King of the Ring, and therefore a lady of some substance in our comically insular little world.

For Ralton's birthday, I'd bought him a new BMX. It had taken me two hours, a whole reel of Scotch tape and three rolls of gift wrap to cover it. When he got home from the Library, I was sitting in the sun outside our new RV, drinking a beer and reading one of his textbooks, the bike propped against the truck behind me. When he saw it, he stopped, stared, dropped his backpack and ran forward, ripping two huge channels down the paper to reveal the shape no amount of wrapping could disguise. When he saw it was new, and just for him, he stood in front of it and bawled like a four-year-old, with eyes tight shut and mouth wide open.

His caterwauling brought a horrified Mrs Cole out of her RV and straight across the lot to take Ralton in her arms and rock him like a baby against her capacious chest. Ralton shut up crying instantly, grinned from ear to ear, but nonetheless made sure to sniff, snivel and snuggle in as close as he could get. I sat in my lawn chair, smirked, and enjoyed the show. It appeared the gooky little bastard had picked up a thing or two from watching his swaggering big brother play the field. Aggressively accusing me of upsetting my child, and fronting up in preparation for the fight she believed was brewing over my lax parenting style, all the wind was taken from her sails by Ralton artlessly removing his face from her cleavage to upturn puppy-dog eyes and enquire, "Are you a supermodel?" Taken aback, Mrs Cole questioned why he would say such a thing. Ralton clobbered the impressive home run, "Because you're *so* beautiful."

Quite at a loss how to respond to such sweetness, Mrs Cole folded him back into her ample bosom and turned to expend her pent-up indignation upon the man she'd long assumed was his irresponsible rake of a wise-guy Dad. Between us, we sought to put her straight.

I chivalrously offered her the only lawn chair and a cold beer. Ralton fetched her a slice of his birthday cake, and as he practised tricks on his new bike to impress her, I provided Mrs Melanie Cole with a quick rundown of our true circumstances, thereby clarifying Ralton's extreme reaction to his birthday gift and quashing all the rumours clearly circulating about us. She listened without interruption, and with the hint of tears glistening in her very blue eyes.

Melanie Cole turned out to be far from a vacuous trophy wife. She was compassionate, chatty, engaging, just a little bit flirtatious, and nobody's fool. Out of high school and going nowhere, she'd swiftly got her manicured talons into the upwardly-mobile Jesse Cole, and hadn't let go. The deal was to start in rodeo, before attempting to break into professional bullriding with its huge earning potential. On hitting thirty, the faithful and patient Melanie would be rewarded with a baby and a house. She wouldn't complain about more than a decade living in an RV with no social life, dirt, dust and everything stinking of manure, and he would upkeep his end of the bargain when the time came.

I confessed hero-worship of Jesse and, tipsy on beer and sunshine, she revealed a staggering secret, that Jesse Cole was jealous of *me*! Shy, socially-awkward, with an unfortunate stutter of which he was ashamed, monosyllabic ice-man Jesse would have apparently given his right arm for an ounce of my easy-going charm, and fluency and wit down the compere's microphone. By the time Mrs Melanie Cole wobbled out of my lawn chair, smeared Ralton's cheek with a drunken birthday kiss and tottered off in her kitten heels, we two were firm friends with shared secrets, and Ralton was as head over heels as only a teenager can be.

****

It was a new town and the routine of another competition weekend. Ralton and I were in the diner closest to the rodeo ground. We'd had a steak and fries, and Ralton was settling to his distance-learning project, carefully drawing diagrams in his geography report with characteristic concentration and precision. I was drinking my coffee, staring out of the window watching the world go by, silently patting myself on the back at how well we were doing, when the darkly-clad figure of none other than Jesse Cole himself slid into our booth. He very slowly and deliberately removed his hat, ran a square palm through his crew-cut, nodded at the waitress to bring him a coffee and lit a cigarette, not uttering a word. It struck me Jesse Cole did everything as if he was auditioning for a Western, and I had to pretend to cough to disguise a sudden fit of the giggles. He hadn't seemed quite so impenetrable since my cosy sunset confessional with his better half the weekend before.

The waitress poured his coffee. He pulled the ashtray closer. I wondered aloud whether Mr Cole was present to assist with the geography project. He replied slowly, deliberately, that he was no professor. He was there to request I desist from making advances towards his wife; namely, the bunches of freshly-picked wildflowers on the RV steps in the mornings, carefully-copied love poems on little slips of paper tucked between the stems.

Laughing, I explained he'd got the wrong guy, and if he wanted to look anywhere for Melanie's secret admirer, it should be eighteen inches to my left. Mortified, Ralton tried to kick my ankles under the table. The merest flicker of a smirk traversed the usually-impassive features of Jesse Cole, but he dragged heavily on his cigarette, regarded the two of us through squinting eyes and said nothing. At length, "Three hours to drive here last night, and she did nothing but talk about *you* the whole damn way. What am I supposed to make of that?"

"Ah, so it's okay for *Ralton* to hit on your wife, just not me? You wanna be careful. I bet his dick's bigger'n yours, *and* he can impress her with his diagrams."

Ice-man pressed his thin lips together, but there was a definite crinkling of the skin around his eyes. I pushed my luck, "Way I see it, it's only a matter of time. He'll be peddling her off on his BMX before you can say 'wet dream'."

The lips twitched. The cool eyes danced momentarily.

I tried a different tack, "You know, this pantomime villain shit's making us a lot of money, huh? Quite a double-act we're turning out to be. But you realise the plucky underdog always wins in the end, right?"

An unimpressed lifting of one eyebrow, and Jesse Cole picked up his hat and slid from the booth without another word. He spent a while at the counter. I figured he was settling up for his coffee, but five minutes later the waitress came over with desserts we hadn't ordered. Ralton's was an ice-cream sundae with a 'Happy Birthday' sparkler, and mine was a chocolate brownie with the words 'Fuck You' expertly piped across the top in vanilla icing. The waitress shrugged sheepishly in an 'I-just-dish-it-out-and-clear-it-up' kinda way. Oh, and when I went to pay, I found he'd already bought our steaks too. That was the start of a friendship I'm certain will see us to our graves – and you know he still doesn't say much, even thirty years later.

****

We cried like babies the day Ralton graduated from University. I stood in my best suit with Jesse and Mel beside me, all of us bawling, and Ralton on stage in his robe and mortar, blushing at the show we were making.

When a big oil company accepted Ralton on their management-training scheme and he packed up and went to live in Texas, I missed him terribly but knew he'd make it. Aside from the bottomless love he'd always have from me, I could do no more. It was up to him now. I'd fulfilled my promise to Mom. At thirty-two, it looked as if my own life could finally begin.

Instead of just recreational flirting and casual sex, I tried to take it seriously, go on dates, make more of an effort to get to know the women who showed an interest in me. That was when I discovered how difficult it was to get close to anybody. I moved around so much that keeping in touch was tricky. They didn't want a long-distance romance, nor did they want to travel with me. Even the unmarried ones had homes, lives, jobs, ties, and they didn't want to break them. I came to understand how precious Melanie was to Jesse. She'd been the only one prepared to sacrifice a normal life in pursuit of his career.

I felt for the two of them, my best friends. Five years older, the deal had always been to try for a baby age thirty, and quit our crazy, peripatetic life once the happy event occurred. Thirty came and went for Jesse and Mel, and thirty-one, and thirty-two, and on, and on...

When forty passed, Jesse was still competing and Mel still wasn't a Mom, you could see the toll it was taking on both of them. When Ralton married his University sweetheart, Jennifer, and they announced there was a baby on the way, to her credit Melanie got the champagne out and put on the bravest face you've ever seen, but we could all read the pain in her eyes. The injury that ripped my shoulder to pieces and finished my career ironically ended up fixing us all.

****

Once I quit the circuit, it took away Jesse's final reason to keep riding on, year after year. We were the last of the old guard against what seemed like a bunch of teenagers, and every bump, scrape, tear and pull took three times longer to recover from. The day after an event, it'd take us five minutes of wincing and cracking just to get up out of a chair.

When the surgeon said he'd put as much of my shoulder back together as he could but that I'd never compete again, there was no choice. I was thirty-seven. I had to find something to do with the rest of my life. Jesse and Mel bought a little house with a few acres. I parked my RV in their paddock, paid them ground rent, did my physiotherapy exercises and worried about the future. All I knew was horses and showing off. Jesse and I would sit on a log under the trees next to the RV, throw stones at towers of empty beer cans, and rack our brains…

Ralton and Jen came to visit, bringing the amazing scan pictures of their growing baby. Melanie hugged Ralton with undiminished devotion, smiled fit to crack her face in two, pleaded a migraine, retired to her bedroom, and none of us judged her for it. Jen – tired, hot, nauseous – went in the RV for a snooze. That left Jesse, Ralton and I yawning in the sultry shade, talking crap to keep Jesse's mind off that scan picture, the perfect little baby it wasn't Ralton and Jen's fault they'd had the good fortune to create.

Ralton was spouting some anecdote about a bunch of desk-jockeys from his firm that'd gone on a dude ranching cattle drive for a bachelor party. They'd returned to the office a long-weekend later like the walking wounded, with black eyes, split lips, one guy in a sling, another on crutches, but all universally delighted with the 'authenticity' of the whole experience, desperate to return at the earliest opportunity to half-kill themselves all over again. While Jesse and Ralton chuckled away, my brain started firing. All you needed was some good grazing, accommodation, some stabling, maybe a barn or two. Get the city-slickers to rough it, and Jesse and I could do what we did best, spend all day in the saddle showing off for a living. We wouldn't even have to break a sweat!

****

It was easy to convince Jesse to sell their house. He hated being stuck in one place with nothing to do, and Mel was a shadow of her former, feisty self these days, meekly following along with our crazy scheme as if she didn't really care one way or another. It took a while to find the right place, but when we three stood on that ridge in Wyoming and stared out across the wide-open prairie below us, simultaneously we all knew we were home.

We planned, grafted, made mistakes, learned from them, did things better. We sank every penny we had into building our futures. We offered all the traditional stuff like learning to ride, trekking in the forest and across the prairie, camping out by the waterfall, but such was the residual pedigree of Jesse Cole, we also sponsored boys to compete on the professional circuit. We had dramatic competition photographs of us plastered all over the lodge, and our stack of rodeo trophies and bullriding buckles in a huge cabinet by Reception.

You didn't have to love the cowboy life to stay with us. Some people came purely to support our philosophy. Journalists wrote about our ethos and the 'pay-it-forward' lifestyle we espoused. Celebrities had their photographs taken by our waterfall. Melanie filled an album with her beaming next to various A-Listers on the steps of our lodge. It didn't matter *why* they came. It was just important that they kept *on* coming, and told all their rich buddies too. With three years of only red on the balance sheet as we planted, sweated and slogged, when we sat down with the accountant after our first full year of trading, we discovered we were in the black all the way. Without so much as one qualification between us, we were becoming successful entrepreneurs.

Jesse and I bowled back into his kitchen full of ourselves, ready to make inroads into the bourbon and fill Mel in on the best (and first) such business meeting we'd ever attended, only to be brought up short by the sight of her, sitting still and silent at the kitchen table, hands demurely in her lap. Expressionless, she placed a flat plastic straw on the table top. There were two windows in its centre, and a thick blue line cut through the middle of each. Not accustomed to the sight of a pregnancy test, I didn't know what it was at first, but Jesse did, and he knew what two blue lines meant. I'd never heard him yell so loud. He picked her up off the chair and whirled her round and round the kitchen while she laughed and screamed at him to stop. Eventually, after the hugs, the congratulations and the bourbon, of course, I left them chewing each other's faces off and wandered down the path to the river.

The sun was dropping behind the far mountains as I crouched on the shoreside pebbles and trailed my fingers in the cold, clear water. I looked up to catch the last rays of the setting sun on my face and considered that, truly, life couldn't get any better. Why, then, did I feel so unfulfilled?

PART III:

'The TV Gold'

EVERETT

"Not *more* interviews!"

I hold the door open for her, "No, this our room for tonight. They're meant to have moved our stuff earlier while we were downstairs."

"How do you know all this?"

"I asked whatsisname, Vasquez. Didn't you notice?"

She frowns, sheepish, "No. Too busy wondering when I might get to take off these instruments of torture masquerading as shoes!"

I can't help grinning at her accent, the comical way she talks, "The good news is there's no cameras until tomorrow apparently, so you can take off whatever you want!"

"Thank Christ for that!"

She immediately bends down right in front of me to slip off the high heels. I have to resist the instant temptation to slide my hands around her hips. So far, I've done only the minimum amount of socially-acceptable touching: holding her hand during the ceremony when instructed by the Celebrant, an arm about her waist when directed by the photographer. Are we being encouraged to do more now? She's a stranger...and my wife...and they've put us in this plush hotel suite for our first night together. What do they want to happen?

She's already gliding away from me, down the hall and into the suite, front of her long gown gathered up in her hands. The lace train streams across the carpet behind her. I kick off my own shoes carelessly and swiftly follow. She stops in the middle of the spacious lounge and curls her toes into the tufted rug, "Ohhh, that's so much better! They were starting to *burn*..."

I notice the straps of the shoes have left deep indentations across the tops of her tiny feet, "Sure glad I'm not a girl. Couldn't do the footwear."

She sniggers, "I'm quite glad you're not a girl too, or I've signed up for the wrong sort of show!"

"Why do you ladies put yourselves through the agony?"

"Because…" She turns, pads back, stands in front of me, body inches from mine. In amazement, I realise quite how little she is. The crown of her head is level with my collarbone. She upturns her face, "See?"

I want to touch her. My mind is empty of everything else. I can't even remember what we were talking about. I burble, "Definitely no cameras in here?"

She turns from me, moves away, rescues me from the building pressure of my desire, "Can't see any…"

"You've gotta look everywhere for the glint of a lens…"

"Are you telling me you don't trust Vasquez, your new tv bestie?" Her eyes twinkle.

I grin, "Not an inch."

"I reckon you're right to be suspicious. They'll do anything for an angle…"

"There's probably a clause in the small print reserving the right to lie blatantly to us for the purposes of entertainment."

"How cynical! How probably accurate! I can't see anything that looks like a camera."

"Nor can I. Okay, perhaps we'll give them the benefit of the doubt and act like no one's filming."

"Which is what we're supposed to do anyway. You're very good at that, I've noticed, acting natural when there's ten cameras in your face."

"I refuse to let this turn me into something I'm not."

"I wish I could ignore them. I can't forget they're there."

"You'll figure it out."

"Hope so." She yawns wide, "Oh, I'm shattered…"

"Me too. I guess it's delayed stress."

"That's weddings for you! I seem to recall being wiped-out after the first one as well. Oh…"

"You've been married before?"

The watchful eyes fix on mine, "Is that a problem?"

"No. That's life."

"How about you?"

"Never."

"Never been tempted?"

"Never had the chance! That's why I'm here. I always wanted a wife, but I could never figure out how to get one…"

She doesn't respond, just watches me with those very green eyes. We're standing in the middle of this fancy suite five feet from one another, edgy and awkward like we've just been introduced at a party, "How 'bout I fix us a drink and we can kick back and talk? You can tell me about your first wedding."

She gapes, "You want to know about my *ex-husband*?"

"I want to know why you're here, doing this. I want to find out what makes you tick."

Her gorgeous smile is wide. Her eyes shine. Perhaps plain old neglect broke up the first marriage?

I go to the kitchen area. On the way, I lose my jacket, waistcoat, tie. I'm not accustomed to being this buttoned-up for quite so long. I examine the contents of the fridge and pick through the overflowing basket of goodies on the small countertop. Should I tell her there's a bottle of champagne chilling, or will she assume I just want to get her drunk?

"You want a *drink* drink, or a soda or something?" If she wants a real drink, then I'm popping this cork and taking full advantage of whatever ensues.

She yawns again, "I can't have booze, I'll go to sleep! Please may I have a coffee?"

"Sure." No booze. Tough luck, Everett, it's not going to go that way. She curls on one end of the couch and tucks her feet under her, rubbing them absently. I make the drinks and walk over. She takes up so little room I figure it's okay to sit next to her. I rest my aching head against the back of the couch, cradle my cup against my chest, put my feet up on the coffee table, "So, tell me about your first marriage."

A hard expression settles. She reaches forward for her coffee, cups the big mug in both hands, takes a couple of dainty sips of the too-hot liquid, "What do you want to know?"

"About your life before now. About why he isn't still your husband."

"Oh, that's easy enough!" She tries to assume a breezy tone, but her voice catches, "He wanted babies, and I couldn't have them. Justin always achieved exactly what he set out to do. He got pissed off at me for ruining all his meticulous planning. He moved in someone who was less of a failure."

"Ah."

"Yeah."

"And the replacement?"

"Positively embryonic. Legs up to here. Hair down to there. Your basic husband-nicking nightmare."

"How old were you when you got married?"

"Twenty-one."

"Is that too young?"

"Probably. I dropped out of my degree to marry him."

"Do you regret that?"

"Maybe. Hard to write the counterfactual, isn't it? I might have attained every career distinction under the sun and still ultimately ended up on the heap for failing to produce the requisite quota of offspring."

"I guess. Gotta play the hand you're dealt. What did they say was wrong?"

"With me? Nothing…or everything..? They never could find anything in particular…but something is, isn't it, or we wouldn't be here having this conversation."

"You'd still be Justin's wife. The mother of his children."

"I expect I would." At least she's honest about it.

"How about you? Didn't you want to be a Dad?"

I wonder how best to answer, "I sort of *was* a Dad. I brought up my little brother after my Mom died, so I do have experience of raising a kid. Just not *my* kid."

She yawns again, rubbing her knuckles into her watering eyes, smudging mascara across her cheeks.

Not thinking, I murmur gently, "Let's go to bed."

Suddenly she's wide awake. A hint of my yearning for her must have crept into my voice, as she's looking at me with an expression that wasn't there a second ago.

"How many beds are in this suite?"

I'm not going to apologise for desiring her. She's a beautiful woman. She's my wife. But I also don't want to make this a big deal. Shrugging, closing my eyes again, I suggest, "I'm guessing, one?"

I peek at her. She stands quickly, "Talk about chuck us in at the deep end!"

She peers into the dark bedroom, "Yeah, our stuff *is* in here…and there's only one bed."

She fidgets in the doorway, unconsciously hugging her arms around herself, "Do you think they expect us to do it?"

"I don't know *what* they expect…"

"Um…*could* you do it?"

I lift my head and look steadily at her, "Yes, I could."

She blinks, perhaps taken aback by the directness of my answer.

"Oh…"

I put myself in her shoes. I'm a big guy. She's a tiny woman. If I were to decide I wanted something she didn't care to give…? It makes me think of my Mom and Parker and that final night in the trailer. I turn my face away. The idea I might be behaving even remotely like Martin Parker disturbs me beyond rational explanation, "Forget it, Hope. I'm sleeping on the couch."

She reacts instantly, "You can't! Your feet will hang off the end! You'll have a terrible night. *I* should sleep on it."

"No, Hope – "

"But I'll fit!"

I want to say, 'no wife of mine is sleeping on a couch', but know it sounds ridiculous.

She fidgets more, "Do you think I'm being a prude?"

"Not at all."

"Um…it's a really massive bed. How about we agree to stick to our own sides for tonight? That way we both get a decent rest, but it's not…you know… Is that a solution?" Concern clouds her features. In that moment, I find myself repulsive: big, male and threatening.

"You're safe with me, Hope. Truly you are. I will never make you do something you don't want to, okay?"

She smiles shyly, "Thank you. I appreciate that," and I feel like an asshole for implying I've done her some kind of favour. Being a guy sucks sometimes.

I get up, walk over to her, take her hand and hold it gently, "Let's get some rest, like you said."

She squeezes my fingers, "Yes, please."

"Okay."

"I need a shower," she rubs at her smudged eyes and examines the smear of make-up across her fingertips, "I want to wash all this horrible goop off."

"I could do with one as well. Those tv lights make you feel like a damp rag." I tug my pyjamas clear of the tangle of my bag.

Kneeling on the floor, a fragile figure in a puddled swirl of lace, she unzips her small suitcase. She seems agitated and, yes, she's definitely trembling. I sit on the chaise at the end of the bed, several feet away, "Hope, you okay?"

She jumps as if I've shouted in her ear, whipping the lid down on her half-empty case. It strikes me its contents are rather meagre. Is that all she's brought with her from England?

"What's wrong?"

She's blushing, stuttering, glancing behind her to check she's closed the lid. She places one small hand on it to reassure herself it can't flip open and reveal what's inside, "I've…forgotten my nightclothes. I've left them in England. I've nothing to sleep in!"

Oh Lord, I can't lie placidly next to her knowing she's naked!

I toss my pyjama top at her. She catches it in surprise, "I'll wear the bottoms, you wear the top. It'll be like a dress on you, anyway. It's clean. It only looks like a rag 'cos I'm not too hot at packing…"

She gazes at me, the creased top clutched in her fists.

"You want first shower, or shall I?"

She beams up at me, "You can. I need to take all the pins out of my hair."

****

When I emerge from the bathroom, the wedding-gown is folded neatly across the back of the chaise and my new wife is already in my pyjama top. Mrs McCann doesn't immediately notice me. She's settled on the pile of pillows against the headboard, sleepily unpinning the ring of silk flowers from her long hair, eyes closed. The loose V-neck has slipped to reveal the creamy flesh of one shoulder. Her legs are curled underneath her as they were on the couch. The hem of the top has ridden up to expose the length of one smooth thigh all the way to the buttock. I stop on the threshold, grip the doorjamb on either side, "You're asleep already."

"Nearly..." Hooded eyes, dreamy voice, slim little fingers combing rhythmically through her hair, searching for stray pins. I'm so turned on by it all I don't know what to do with myself. I try to fight the arousal, picture my Mom being brutalised by Parker – the guaranteed passion-killer – but the memory won't come. What surfaces instead is the sight of Hope standing next to me at the altar, edible body barely concealed by net and lace, smiling hesitantly as our eyes meet.

I want her. I want her with every fibre of my being and I want her *now*...and I can't have her because I've promised I won't touch. What kind of a marriage will it be if I break my first vow within half an hour of making it?

My treacherous brain pictures me reaching for her ankles, tugging them, the pyjama top sliding up as I ease her across the mattress towards me.

I sit down on the edge of the bed, flapping the covers back across my lap and cursing my lack of self-control.

She asks, "Which side do you usually sleep?"

There are sides? I shrug, "In the middle."

She laughs as if I'm kidding, "Only I'm used to sleeping on the left. It's so ingrained I even sleep on the left in an empty bed…so I'd like to sleep on the left if it's okay with you." My free-spirited upbringing rebels against such conventions, "It's fine, Hope. You sleep on the left, I'll sleep in the middle."

As I turn to take off my watch and put it on the nearest nightstand, she sees the scars on my back, the criss-cross of damaged tissue from the three operations to rebuild my shattered shoulder.

"Ow! Are they from the same fight?"

"No…no… That's from an injury that finished my previous sports career. There's more metalwork in there than the Golden Gate Bridge."

"Does it hurt?"

"Used to only bother me in the winter time, but just recently it's starting to ache more and more. Probably an age thing."

I instantly regret saying that. She'll think I'm past-it, complaining about my aches and pains. I burrow into the bed and curl up to disguise my arousal from her. It's a relief to rest my buzzing head, "I can't believe how tired I am. It's been the weirdest day of my whole life…"

"You can say that again!"

I wink at her, "It's late. Go have your shower."

I deliberately keep my back to her as she walks to the bathroom. I spend five minutes fretting about how I'll sleep a wink knowing she's within reach, before exhaustion claims me. I'm snoring deeply before Mrs McCann is even out of the shower.

HOPE

Blinking blearily across a huge room in semi-darkness, I feel groggy and confused. I can't work out exactly where I am. Something tells me I should know, but I feel too sluggish and snug to bother reasoning it out. It *is* strange the skirting seems so very far away... I've got used to the walls of my tiny bedsit being incredibly close to my fuzzy eyes as I squint into the half-light of another early morning, irritated by the wheep of the alarm clock. I feel drunk with slumber. I'm so *warm*. I haven't felt this rested in years...

Although I'm barely awake, my full bladder starts to niggle. I make a half-hearted attempt at movement, only to discover I can't budge. Hot solidity at my back. Rhythmic, moist breath against the nape of my neck. The weight of a massive arm like a felled tree across my body. I remember yesterday with a jolt, realising the borrowed pyjama top has ridden up and is bunched around my waist! My naked buttocks are pressed against Everett's stomach. Wide awake now, I frantically try to free an arm, but his big, relaxed limb is a dead weight on top of me. Experimental wriggling only succeeds in making the top ride higher, exposing more naked me to contact with his warm torso. It's not unpleasant, but this is way too intimate a position to be in with a virtual stranger, however unconventional the circumstances. My fidgeting stirs Everett, who murmurs and hugs me more tightly to him as his muscles tense and his breathing shallows. He wakes with a low grunt like a grumpy bear. I lie quite still and hold my breath while he processes this most unfamiliar situation. A gasp and instant rush of cold air as he jerks away from me across the wide mattress, hissing, "Shit!"

I seize the chance to yank the pyjama top back down. Deciding I can't fake waking up convincingly enough not to look an idiot, I roll onto my back. He's watching me warily, a guilty look on his face. My own bashfulness at the skin-to-skin contact fades in the face of his obvious mortification.

"I'm sorry. I didn't do anything, I promise! I must've got cold in the night and just gravitated towards you."

"You did tell me you were going to sleep in the middle."

I try to let him off the hook as gently as he'd rescued me from the humiliation over my nightclothes, "I was really warm. It's the best I've slept in years."

He smiles, relief in his eyes, "I slept good too. I was having a lovely dream I was floating down the river at home with the sun on me."

"So, you live by a river…?"

"I shouldn't have said that, should I? It's meant to be a surprise when you get there. I don't want to be told off by scary Producer Rachel for breaking the rules!"

We're facing one another, but there's a respectable expanse of divan between our bodies, "Can you at least tell me about your shoulder injury…your past career?"

"I used to ride saddle bronc in the rodeo…and then I was a pro bullrider, but my shoulder injury meant I had to give that up."

"Can you make money at that?"

"Oh, sure. Quite a lot of money! Danger money. I got hurt before I felt my time was really up. Wasn't my choice to stop when I did, but I had to quit."

"How long ago?"

"Twelve years."

"What have you done since then?"

"I'm not allowed to *tell* you! Rachel will rap my knuckles with her clipboard!"

"Give me a clue!" I whine.

"No. You have to guess."

"Right. Are you a lifeguard?"

"What?" He starts laughing, which sets me off as well. A funny feeling bubbles inside me. Nervous excitement, as if I'm preparing to skydive.

"Why a lifeguard?"

Blushing, stammering, "You've got a gorgeous bod and a lovely tan."

He's still laughing, "You're gonna get such a shock. Where we're going sure ain't Malibu."

"But you have an outdoorsy job…?"

"Yeah, I do…but I'm not in *Baywatch*."

"Put me out of my misery! You can give me a hint without doing details…"

"Okay. I'm a farmer."

"I can't believe I didn't think of that."

"Yeah…that your brain went, route one: lifeguard."

We lie still, three feet apart, eyes raking what we can see of one another, nervously smiling when we're caught staring. Hesitantly, Everett asks, "You don't mind…about the scar on my face or the mess of my shoulder?"

His body is delectable, but it feels a bit what my mother would call *forward* to blurt that out. I opt for the tamer, "You're very handsome, Everett, and you're in fantastic physical shape."

He chuckles, gratified, "So you're not revolted by the battering my body's taken?"

"Of course not! You seem to have had a pretty eventful life."

"I sure have…and it's getting more exciting by the minute."

I'm gurning like the proverbial village idiot, but he's grinning back just as broadly.

"If we're having this kind of conversation, what about me? Did I look ridiculous in that dress they put me in?"

"Hope, you looked knockout in that dress! I can't believe my luck, honestly."

Oh, I'm embarrassed now. I feel all hot and don't know where to look. To escape, I stammer, "It's my turn to make the drinks."

I edge out of bed, gripping the hem of the pyjama top tight to prevent it riding up again, scuttling quickly to the bathroom. I wash my hands and linger before the large mirror, thinking about the reassuring warm weight of Everett against me. That peculiar, skittery sensation flutters my insides again.

I jump as the door opens. Reflected in the mirror, the delicious definition of Everett's body is highlighted by the brightness of the overhead light, the burnished bronze of his skin making the grey-streaked blonde hair seem lighter, and his eyes a more vivid blue. His powerful torso is broad, and prominent veins traverse his thick neck and strong arms. His appetising abdominal muscles are solid and chunky, immediately conjuring comparison with a chocolate bar; scrumptious, brown, smooth and tempting.

What is he *doing* in here?

He takes another step towards me, "Sorry. I did knock. You didn't answer. I really have to pee."

Relieved and disappointed, I trill, "It's fine! I'll go and put the kettle on."

As I draw level with him, hot fingertips brush and press my forearm, stilling me momentarily. One roughened finger hooks underneath the hem of the pyjama top, drawing it up my thigh almost to my hipbone. The touch tickles, stings, burns and freezes all at once, my body shuddering in petrified anticipation. The encounter lasts perhaps two seconds before I blush an attractive shade of puce and leg it out of the bathroom as fast as my little legs will carry me.

EVERETT

The plane banks and I slouch in my seat, stretching out my legs as much as I can, doing my best to ignore the black square of camera lens peeking surreptitiously between the seats in front. Only diminutive Hope could make the limited space of an airplane seat seem like an armchair as she leans back, unclasps her seatbelt, slips off her shoes and sits cross-legged, knees propped on the armrests.

She's smiling at me. I can't help but smile back. We've spent a lot of the past twenty-four hours doing just this, grinning and gazing, drinking each other in, incapable of articulating our amazement in any other way.

"I'm a bit nervous about meeting your family."

"I can't wait to see their faces. They're gonna be blown away by this."

"What if they don't like me?"

"It'll be fine, Hope."

"Do you think they'll wonder whether you've lost your marbles?"

"I've always been a little bit 'out there'. They'll probably conclude it's just another stunt."

"What other crazy things have you done?"

"Oh, all sorts! When I was young, I had to find quick ways of earning money, so I got accustomed to taking risks. In its way, this is just another one to add to the list."

"Why did you do it, Everett? What made you fill in that form?"

"Loneliness, that's all. From the outside, I have everything I need, but there's this yawning gap I just can't fill with work, or money, or... Does that make sense?"

"I think so."

"Why did *you* do it?"

"I was the ultimate freeloader. In my head, I justified it by reasoning the scales would balance once the babies came along. I'd earn my keep then, and no mistake! It wouldn't be all on Justin any more. We'd be a proper team, and that whole undercurrent of resentment nibbling at the edges of everything would disappear for good."

"But no babies came…"

"It's no wonder Justin got the fat hump with me! If the roles were reversed, I'd have been whingeing *years* before he did."

"He didn't whinge, though. He cheated, right?"

Hope shrugs, "Whatever I think of his new wife, at least she has a job. She earns her own money and contributes, which is more than I ever did. I stuck my head in the sand until it was too damn late, and ended up forty, divorced, homeless, penniless…and I had to drag myself up by my bootstraps and start again. This time, in the *real* world, without anyone to protect me from all the dignity you haemorrhage just scrabbling to get by. I learned so much in such a short time. About myself, about life, about my limitations…but I also discovered that I could dig in and *endure*. When I saw that leaflet, I thought if I could get on the show, I could stick anything for a year, because I'd been living two years of hell already… So I came here for the money, pure and simple. I'm ashamed to admit that, but it's the truth. I had no expectations of this beyond making the best of a doubtless-bad situation, and slogging through to the cash a year from now."

Here, her very green eyes fix unblinkingly on mine, "And then they married me to you."

My sinking heart, dropping like a stone back down through the clouds towards New York without a parachute, stutters in its death-dive of despair and decides to hang ten, optimistically surfing the swirling thermals above the city because there's something in her voice, her face, those eyes…

"I realise we know stuff-all about one another, but already you seem the kindest, most genuine man I've ever met. I'm no longer just escaping my past by being here. I'm contemplating a future!"

HOPE

My heart's pounding as we pull the hire car up outside Everett's brother's house and all pile out.

We scuttle along the drive to crouch behind a large SUV parked halfway up. Everett turns to us, "Okay, y'all stick here behind the car, stay out of sight, and I'll come fetch you in a minute."

He squeezes my hands, grinning, "Don't worry."

The house is in a tree-lined street of detached executive homes with large double garages and post-boxes on sticks at the end of each driveway. Unlike the cramped warrens of terraced housing I'm used to, the expanses of green lawn are as immense as playing fields, the silent street wide and stately. It's a world away from the higgledy-piggledy crush of life in the most crowded corner of my tiny native country.

I duck down at the rear of the large car, camera crew a few feet behind. Slowly, I ease up to peek through the car's rear windows as Everett takes the shallow porch steps in one bound and rings the bell. The door is almost immediately opened by a small brown-haired boy, who takes an instant to register the identity of the caller before squeaking in delight, zooming out, and clamping himself bodily to the visitor's legs, yelling, "Uncle Ev-rett!" in unadulterated joy. Everett effortlessly swings the diminutive assailant high above his head, as a slim, bespectacled blonde appears in the doorway, baby on her hip.

"Ryan! How many times do I have to tell you not to open the – Oh. My. God!" She stops and gawps at her grinning brother-in-law, "What are *you* doing here?"

"And a very good evening to you too, Mrs Parker," Everett points to his cheek, "Where's my sugar?"

Laughing, the woman curls her free arm tight around his neck, and plants a lingering kiss of genuine affection on his cheek. There's more than an air of flirtatiousness about the gesture. A surprising sensation trickles through me: am I *jealous*?

"That's better. Hello, Wendy," stroking the baby's little head gently with his huge palm as she gazes up at him with wide eyes. Ryan is clambering over his uncle, shinning up his body and wriggling onto his back, with little arms around his neck and legs around his waist.

An older boy appears in the doorway beside his mother, also rushing forward into an instant and unselfconscious embrace against his uncle's chest. Everett bends to kiss the top of the boy's head and ruffle his hair.

"I didn't know you were coming to stay!"

"No," Jennifer fixes Everett with gimlet eyes, "Nor did I. What are you up to? Does Ralton know?"

"Nope," Everett can't stop himself smiling.

With laughing exasperation, "Everett, what is going *on*?"

Everett holds up a hand to silence her, walks back down the steps and around behind the Lexus, holding out his hand to me. The camera crew emerge from their vantage point in the bushes. Ryan, still clinging to his uncle's back, yells, "Mommy! There's a lady down here with orange hair, a man making a movie, and another man with some fur on a stick!"

"With *what*?"

Everett steps from behind the car, pulling a cripplingly-bashful me behind him. The camera crew advances across the lawn, microphone boom bouncing over our heads.

"Please don't worry about the camera. It's for a tv show I'm taking part in for a little while. I promise I'll explain it all over the delicious dinner you're going to feed us. *Much* more important than that," Everett edges me gently forward and places a reassuringly-heavy palm on each of my shoulders, "Mrs Parker, meet Mrs McCann."

I smile politely and say, "Delighted to meet you, Jennifer," in my very best telephone voice. My new sister-in-law's eyes become so round and wide I fear they might pop out of her head. She totters back several steps, before clutching the shoulder of her eldest son, and blurting, "Tarryn, go fetch your father!"

EVERETT

On the way back from taking a leak, I'm on the threshold of the kitchen door when Jen's fist grips the front of my shirt and hauls me back inside, hissing, "Are you out of your goddam *mind*?"

I smirk, fold my arms, lean casually against the counter, "Need to get something off your chest, Jenny?"

"You're damn right I do! What do you think, that's she's here because of your sparkling personality?"

I pantomime, "Oh, Jen, is that not *it*?"

Jennifer scowls venomously at me and irritably plonks the baby's bottle into the microwave, slamming the door, "Everett, I accept the whole idea of being in on some kind of off-the-wall social experiment appeals to the truly insane side of your nature, but come *on*!"

Jen parodies Hope's English accent, badly, "Ooh, yes please, Mr Television Producer, I choose the multi-millionaire."

Conscious the object of her suspicion is feet away on the terrace beyond the open kitchen doors, Jennifer points aggressively in the direction of the laughing, chatting group outside, and whispers aggressively, "She's a gold-digger. She's *got* to be! She has her eyes on the prize."

I sigh, suddenly weary of her enmity, of the need to explain and justify what I'm doing.

"Jennifer, no one else in this household seems to have a problem with this. Why do you?"

The microwave beeps and Jen snatches at the door hard enough to loosen hinges, snapping, "Oh pur-*leeese*! The judgement of children, and a man who thinks the sun shines permanently out of your butt no matter what lunacy you engage in? *I'm* the only one thinking about this *rationally*!"

"They're happy that I'm happy, Jen! Why can't that be enough?"

Jen shakes the bottle vigorously under my nose, the mixing formula splashing wildly up the sides of the container, "You have a lot of things a certain type of woman wants. A great deal of money, extensive and valuable property, the requisite level of emotional desperation. You're so caught up in the idea of finally having a wife, you can't see what's staring you in the face! She's already doing the math. You can see it in her eyes. You've done this dumbass thing for real, and you're gonna get taken for everything – "

"How?"

"Huh?"

"How is she going to 'take me for everything'?"

"Wake up! At exactly twelve months and one day, she's in the divorce court suing you for half your fortune!"

"And the pre-nup?"

"*What*?"

Wendy, rendered restless by the long wait for her milk and discomfited by her mother's anger, considers it the final straw to be smothered against Jen's chest as she rounds furiously upon me once more. She begins to cry lustily. Concerned, I reach forward, "Jen, you're upsetting the baby! Calm down so we can talk about this like sensible adults. Give Wendy to me, have a glass of wine, and just *stop*, willya?"

Pouting, she nevertheless allows me to lift little Wendy from her tense grasp and nestle her in the crook of my arm, pushing the teat of the bottle into her already-puckering mouth, cooing comfortingly, "That's better, isn't it, sweet-pea? You hang with Uncle Everett…"

Jen, anger abating somewhat as she watches her daughter, says, "She looks tiny when you hold her."

"She *is* tiny, aren't you, Wendy?"

Jen opens the fridge and takes out a half-consumed bottle of wine, pouring herself a generous glass and knocking back a third in one swallow, muttering, "So, what about this infallible pre-nup, then? I bet you fifty bucks in less than two years your lawyers are battling over every penny you've got."

"Jennifer, I never knew you were such a cynic! The pre-nup lasts for seven years. The only stuff she can get her hands on at twelve months and one day are assets acquired *during* the marriage, which, according to the pre-nup, must be split fifty-fifty…and we both agree with that, because we've both signed it. Anything she or I had before the I do's remains ours alone. I'm hoping after seven years of marriage we'll either have developed some sort of a rapport, or I'll have got wise and kicked her out, won't I, Wendy?"

"You're not taking this seriously enough."

"And you're taking it *too* damn seriously! She's signed a contract to have no claim over anything of mine for seven years, okay? Same as I have no claim over anything of hers. If she leaves me next year, she'll walk away with $500,000 tv prize money that doesn't come out of my pocket, and *nothing* else! Hope has no idea what I have. She has no clue about Ridge River Ranch or *any* of it! Not yet. Beyond telling her I'm a farmer, she knows nothing about me, Jen. Nothing."

"And you know nothing about her."

"And *that* is the point of the show and the reason for the adventure, right there! I do know one thing, she's risking a helluva lot more than I am to do this. She's left her country, her culture, her family, and everything she knows in the world to start a new life with a total stranger. All *I'm* risking is my bachelor existence…and I gotta tell you, Jen, I ain't that attached to it."

"You're letting romance take precedence over responsibility!"

"And what's so wrong with that once in a goddam lifetime? I'm up to here with responsibilities! They're all I've ever *had*, Jen! Don't you think I might *enjoy* a little romance, just this one time?"

"I know life's been tough for you. I fully understand – "

"No, you don't, and you never will! Ralton doesn't even 'fully understand', and he was there for most of it. Tell you what, give Ryan to Tarryn, dump 'em both out in the street with no money and the clothes they stand up in, and leave 'em to survive. Don't write, don't call, don't give a shit…oh, and just when they think you might come back and save 'em, slit your wrists instead without apology or explanation. Getting close to the sensation?"

"…All right, Everett. I *don't* understand."

We glare at one another, and the only sound is the rhythmic, squeaking suck of the baby's lips on the rubber teat, before a gale of laughter from outside distracts us both and I relent, whispering, "I'm sorry. I didn't mean to get annoyed. I just can't see what your problem is with this."

Jen's expression softens. She pulls gently at my shirtsleeve, "My 'problem' is you're gonna get your stupid heart broken! Can you not *see* that?"

HOPE

The chiselled-out lettering of the hanging sign is infilled with gold paint that catches the late afternoon sunlight as the taxi makes its wide turn off the highway. Ridge River Ranch. At the very bottom of the sign, five large stars glint proud of the weather-blackened wood. We bump up the stony track, tyres crunching and popping. It divides in front of us, a narrower trail curling left through leggy sagebrush and close-planted pine. Everett leans forward and taps the driver on the shoulder, "We'll get out here and walk up. Please can you take the left fork and leave the bags outside the farmhouse?" He's doling out the required fare, piling worn and rustling bills onto the driver's outstretched palm. By the time I've fumbled my shoes on he's opening my door, reaching in and handing me out in old-fashioned style. I blush, liking it.

The cab swings to the left and disturbs an eye-prickling cloud of dust as it bounces away up the track. The strength of the sun is intense. I can already feel the warmth through my thin blouse. Everett pats the top of his head, "I miss my hat. Didn't take it to New York."

I touch my own head. It's cooking, "I think I might need to get one."

He looks down at my pumps, already filling with disturbed grit that rubs abrasively at the sides of my feet as I move, "You'll need some boots, too."

He takes my hand, "Come on. I wanted us to walk up the smart way so you can understand everything."

I stumble after him, my impractical city shoes slipping in the shifting, stony dust. The long grass is baked yellow by the intense sunlight, the clumps of sagebrush showing smoky silver. There are wildflowers everywhere. Delicate sprays of white upon which busy insects settle. Star-shaped purple with bright yellow centres. Rosehip, wild raspberry and puffs of cottongrass like miniature dandelion clocks.

My heart is pounding. My chest feels tight. I push a palm to my sternum, "I'm so puffed!"

"We're at about six thousand feet here."

"That'd explain it."

"We'll slow down."

"I'm okay," I pant. "Have to get used to it."

"I wanted to give a good impression of the place, not kill you off on your first day."

Silver birches line the wide drive, papery bark snow white in the sunlight. Their branches meet above us and we pass into a cathedral of golden shade. Rounding a bend, I'm taken aback by the lushness of two huge lawns, vivid in the parched landscape, sweeping away to either side of the tree-lined avenue like fairways on a golf course. At the edge of the ridge, an imposing stone and wood lodge occupies an elevated position above a deep ravine. Beyond, densely-wooded slopes jut skyward with gravity-defying steepness into the hazy sky. The sun glints off rippling water to the rear of the building, "A pool?"

"Yeah. Geothermal. Guests swim when there's snow on the ground."

The five stars on the sign suddenly make sense. "This is a *hotel*?"

"Yes, Ma'am."

"I thought you had a farm? Were you taking the piss? Do you run a hotel?"

"No. Melanie does."

Immediately, I'm gripped by that intense wave of irrational jealousy again. I hear myself squawking, "Who's Melanie?"

"Jesse's wife. You'll see."

With renewed gentle pressure on my elbow, Everett steers me up another fork in the track, signposted 'Corral'. We're still climbing steadily. My heart continues to hammer with unaccustomed exertion. Insects buzz past, cracking like static. Their wings are a striking lemon yellow with purple tips, "What are those funny moths?"

"They're crickets. Watch." Everett's finger trails the nearest one in an erratic helix to the ground, whereupon its wings fold away, the harsh sound ceases, and it becomes a recognisable grey-green grasshopper, feelers waving inquisitively as we lean over and cast a shadow.

Tramping on, Everett explains, "My closest rival when I started competing, who turned into my very best friend in the whole world, is a guy called Jesse Cole, and his wife Melanie. When I got hurt and I couldn't ride any more, Jesse was 'bout ready to retire, 'cos he's older than me, so we talked it over, pooled the money we'd earned, went in fifty-fifty...and we were only going to open a little dude-ranch, but then Melanie got involved and here we are! Goddam five-star luxury and all the trimmings...because she stamped her feet and pouted and both of us were too scared to argue with her. Jesse wanted to keep our toe in the rodeo water, and I wanted us to sell this ethos that you can make a helluva difference without leaving a mark. Put all that together and Ridge River is what you get. Melanie's thing is the hotel, the 'lifestyle' bullshit, the rich guests, the pampering, and she's very good at it. Just don't tell her I said that. Jesse's baby is the stock-breeding, the rodeo school, the mentoring of riders...and my job is to keep it all running: the farm, the food. It works. The three of us rub along okay, and we don't tread on each other's toes. We don't say it much out loud, as if that might break the spell, but we're all quietly proud of what we've done here. It was a tumbledown mess when we bought it."

Another glade of silver birches separates the rear of the hotel gardens from a secluded plot on which a smaller wood and stone house nestles amongst a neglected garden of wonderfully overgrown flowers, alive with butterflies, "That's Jesse and Mel's place. They have a son, Shane. He's nine soon. They waited a long time to be parents, and not through choice, so Mel might understand some of what you felt, the disappointment of wanting to be a Mom and it not happening the way you planned."

"Is Shane adopted?"

"No, he's Jesse's boy through and through. We call it the Ridge River Effect. Must be something in the water. It fixes everybody. My broken boys come here going through a whole heap of shit, and this place just…changes them, irons out all the kinks."

"What do you mean?"

We stop again, this time by an immense dusty square fenced with criss-cross poles like so many tee-pees. The arched gate says 'Corral'. To one side, extensive rows of stabling, and buildings labelled tack room and changing room. Another gate marked 'private' leads further on into the woods.

Several sizeable trailers occupy a large car park. From one, a teenage boy and middle-aged man are unloading a reddish, speckled horse, which the lad leads across the shingle to drink from the enclosure's large water trough. In the distance, I can see the tails of other horses swishing and flicking as they meander between patches of shade cast by spreading trees, long necks bowing to graze.

The older man approaches Everett, who extends a hand, smiling broadly, "Hello, Todd. Jesse looking after you?"

Todd pumps Everett's hand enthusiastically, rolling a cheroot from one side of his mouth to the other with a practised twitch of his lips, "Everett! Good to see you. Yeah, he said he'd be right out."

"Carter ready for his moment of glory?"

Todd sighs heavily, "You never know how they'll perform on the day…"

Everett's smile widens, but I notice he offers no words of comfort to the markedly-tense Todd. I'm still trying to work out whether they're discussing boy or horse. Everett glances across at the petrified-looking teenager, smacks Todd encouragingly on the shoulder, and cautions, "We've got a full book, Todd. He's gotta show Jesse something pretty special."

Todd groans, "No pressure, huh? My wife already says I smoke too much." He grounds out the spent butt under the heel of his boot.

Everett sniggers, "That shit'll kill you, Todd!" and we keep going without waiting for a reply, through the gate and further up the track.

I tug at his sleeve to slow him down, "Explain…?"

"Oh, poor old Todd! What Carter wants, Carter gets…and Carter wants to be a rodeo star, and Todd wants Jesse to get him there. Todd may be rich, but it'll take more money than he's ever seen, and then a bit more! Hell, I could enter *you* in a rodeo tomorrow and you'd score more points than Carter Traynor. He'll shit himself when Jesse arrives to do his assessment. There's nothing in the world more frightening than Mr Cole with his game-face on. It still scares the bejesus outta me, and *I* know he's kidding."

"So, Carter's had a wasted journey?"

"For sure."

"I feel a bit sorry for him."

"Don't. He wants someone to wave a wand and make him a star. Success takes hard graft. Carter's not prepared to work, so he'll never make it."

"Do you turn a lot of people away?"

"Yes, Ma'am."

"You pick your customers?"

"That's Jesse Cole."

"I see."

"He acts intimidating, but really he's cute and cuddly. We're having dinner with them later. I can't wait. They sure won't be expecting you!"

I wonder, with some consternation, exactly what he means.

The sharp steepness of the hill is levelling out. I surmise we must be reaching the top of the ridge. There's a constant rushing away to my right. My city senses assume it's a road beyond the trees, but the forest is so dense up here I can't make it out.

"What did you mean about broken boys?"

"Sorry, I got distracted by Carter-the-hopeless, didn't I? The guys who work for me have all done time in Juve. This is kinda probation for 'em. Break the rules, and back they go."

"Oh… How many break the rules?"

"In twelve years, two."

I'm relieved by that statistic, "That's a decent record."

"They're good kids with bad lives. Everyone's good at something. You just have to take the time to figure out what it is."

"Do they like being here?"

"Better than jail, right? Some just do their stint, get their release, and go. Others stay a year or more. A couple of 'em have been here upwards of four years."

"So you don't make them leave?"

"No. We got a kooky little family going on here. For some of these boys, it's the closest they've ever gotten to being a part of one. They like it. *I* like it. We all live together in one big house, share the chores, rely on one another."

"That's quite sweet."

"I believe in it. I believe in everything we do here. It just illustrates how you don't have to sell your soul to turn a profit."

"You sound like a bit of a hippie."

"I suppose I do…"

We round the final bend in the track and the next vista opens before us. To our left, farmland stretches almost as far as I can see across the valley, the distant highway delineating the horizon, an occasional vehicle crawling along its thin grey ribbon like an insect down a branch. To our right, an explanation for the constant rushing. Not a motorway, but a waterfall! It tumbles and crashes over polished rocks to a fast-flowing, shallow river, slicing through the deep ravine beneath the hotel. On the opposite side of the waterfall, more pine-covered slopes climb precipitously. Everett nods at the far bank, "Bear country."

Before us, there are massive storage barns, and cattle sheds like aircraft hangars. Everywhere I look, fat nut-brown cows mooch through the meadows, chomping rhythmically. The hot air smells of grass and manure.

Everett turns us right, to the ridge, closer to the powerful rumble of that wall of water, to a long, low building squatting on the summit, without doubt delivering the most breathtaking view of any I have seen so far, straight downriver, across vast prairie towards distant mountains, their chunky grey faces now tinged bright pink by the advancing summer sunset.

Outside the house, a few haphazardly-parked, battered-looking pickups. Our bags squat plumply by the door like roosting pigeons.

"Home. Not as bad as you're probably imagining right now, but not five-star, I'm sorry to say."

"Do you have cockroaches?"

"No…?"

"Then it's already better than where I've been living for the past two years."

He's watching me intently, "You ready for this? They all know you're coming, but obviously not what to expect…"

I get the immediate impression he's preparing me. Albeit young, they're convicted criminals. Am I in danger here?

"Do I need to worry about them?"

Everett is quick to shake his head, "No, no…it's not that. They just don't have a filter. Some of the stuff that comes out can be a little shocking. They don't mean any harm by it, but they also don't think before they speak half the time. It's a cross between an orphanage and a zoo in there."

Increasingly nervous, I gulp, "Where are the cameras?" Already, I'm dreading being under observation again.

"In the kitchen, I think…and obviously in our private bit of the house." Everett shifts from foot to foot, gravel crunching under his boots. I feel foolish leaving it so late to begin asking pertinent questions about our living arrangements, and am about to delve deeper when a young, blonde man appears in the doorway in dirty jeans and scuffed boots. His shirt is unbuttoned to reveal a tanned torso and abdominal definition every bit as impressive as Everett's. This life clearly does wonders for the physique. I gawp involuntarily and blush, mortified, as I realise he's caught me staring. Making no attempt to conceal his body from me, the young man stops, scratches his chest with one hand whilst rearranging his genitalia with the other, and appraises me with shameless thoroughness, before turning and roaring into the house, "Hey, you guys! *Mommy's* home!"

EVERETT

Just what I didn't want to happen, Walker barging out of the tack room door in his filthiest jeans, shirt undone, hair sticking out in all directions like it's never seen a comb, deliberately stirring up the sudden simmering tension with a fat slice of characteristic cheek. When he finishes ogling Hope like she's a centrefold and gets around to meeting my eye, his cocksure manner loses some of its swagger. Plumage ruffled, he shuffles backwards to hold the door open for Hope, indicating she should step inside. She edges warily around his stocky form and tiptoes into the dimness of the tack room as if venturing into a dragon's lair. I follow. As I draw level with Walker, I cuff him sharply around the back of the head with the heel of my hand, point behind us into the yard, and growl, "Bags, shithead."

Chastened, rubbing the back of his head vigorously with a grubby palm, he scuttles outside to fetch the luggage. The outer door swings shut behind him and Hope and I are alone in the echoing gloom, redolent with the familiar scents of leather, wax, wood and horse. The walls seem to groan with the dark weight of regimented lines of saddles, swags of rope, piles of rugs, loops of rein and bridle, baskets of gloves and spurs, and the benches, lockers and pegs along one wall where the boys are supposed to leave their oilskins, chaps, coveralls and filthy boots, in a vain attempt to keep the farmhouse clean and tidy. A laminated sign affixed to the inner door bellows: 'NO outdoor gear in the house!'. When I consider how many times a week I have to scream at each one for wearing his work clothes indoors, you'd think none of them could read a word.

Hope is standing perfectly still in the centre of the flagstone floor, scanning with wide eyes. All of this is so familiar to me I barely notice it, but I try to imagine how it appears to Hope, who knows nothing of this way of life. A jumbled collage is tacked up around the internal door leading to the kitchen. Dumb polaroids of the boys pulling faces and clowning around mix with landscapes of the ranch that Tim takes with his expensive camera, shots of topless girls torn from magazines, and the occasional Western witticism. 'Save a horse, ride a cowboy', 'Come back with a Warrant', and 'Rodeo: because football, baseball, bowling and golf only require one ball'. It's determinedly masculine. I wonder what she must make of it all.

She glances nervously back at me and I smile and nod. Noticeably-shaking fingers reach for the handle, the heavy door swinging open to reveal the large kitchen crammed with intimidating strangers who instantly stop what they're doing, turn as one, and regard Hope with brazen and hostile curiosity.

Between the producers and I, what we've done to poor Hope is undoubtedly great television – her current expression is doubtless worth the annual subscription alone – but it's not exactly an acceptable way to treat one's bride. Ashamed to have gone along so readily with the plan to keep Hope in the dark about what awaited her, guiltily and belatedly protective, I grip her hand firmly. Her small palm is cold and clammy. Gently, I rub my thumb across her knuckles and her trembling fingers twitch against mine.

Nobody moves.

The boys sit, stand, slouch and lean, staring at Hope with frank fascination. The awkward silence is shattered by Walker, thumping in behind us with the cases and stomping moodily off down the hall. His huffing sulkiness makes me snigger, and my uncharacteristic shyness vanishes. Whatever's happened over the last few days, this remains *my* roost, and I fuckin' *rule* it.

I lead Hope across the room, the heads swivelling with our passage like hungry owls tracking a plump dormouse. I pull out the chair at the far end of the table and invite Hope to sit down. She slides stiffly into the high-backed wooden seat, her lips pressed primly together. I continue to grasp her hand and those big, green eyes seek mine, imploring me not to abandon her. I smile encouragingly, survey our audience, and order quietly, "Everybody siddown."

There's a moment of hesitation, which irritates me, so I bark, "Y'all *deaf?*"

They sit, with a shuffling of feet, bumping of bodies and scraping of furniture as all race not to be the last to comply, frantically hooking gangly legs over the benches on either side of the table, jostling one another for room. Not a word is uttered.

I squeeze Hope's hand, release it gently, and walk to the other end of the table, sitting calmly in my accustomed seat at its head. Seven pairs of eyes are fixed unblinkingly upon me.

I grin down the table at my timid wife, "Guys, this is Hope. Hope, I don't expect you to remember, but this is…" I point to each in turn as I go around the table introducing them. To my relief and pride, each tips his hat or tugs his cowlick with a polite and earnest, "Ma'am." I can't believe how well they're behaving. I was fully-expecting Walker's insolence to have infected them all.

"Mo, Bobby, Tim, Hedge, Nathan, Alex…and you'll be pleased to know you aren't usually the only woman here, because our other veterinary intern is Rosemary, Walker's girlfriend. She's away visiting her folks, which is obviously why he thinks it's okay to behave like a Neanderthal."

On cue, Walker reappears in the doorway to a ripple of tittering from the others, all mightily relieved not to have been the one singled-out for ridicule.

"Do your shirt up," I growl.

"Huh? Oh…right…" He buttons swiftly, approaching the table and nudging the others along so he can sit down. Once Walker is settled and no longer providing her with welcome respite, the attention swiftly returns to Hope. I wait to see what she'll do about it, whether eventually she'll reach saturation point and yell at them to quit it, but she appears frozen, unable to do anything but stare fearfully back, anxious eyes flitting restlessly from one expressionless face to the next. I see it's up to me to rescue her, and roar loud enough to make them all jump, Hope included, "Quit gawking! How would y'all like it if everyone stared at *you* and didn't say a damn word!"

Instantly, they're coughing, fidgeting, mumbling; looking at each other, the table top, the ceiling, the dirt under their fingernails...anywhere but at Hope. I roll my eyes, shake my head, lean back in my chair, "Jeez, what a homecoming! We've just gotten married and not one of you has said so much as 'Congratulations'! In fact, no one's said a word except him," I jerk a thumb at Walker, "and what he said was downright rude."

Walker protests, unwisely, "Hey, I got the bags in, didn't I? Anyway, you called me 'shithead'!"

I raise my eyebrows at him. Backchat is not permitted unless I'm in a good mood, and Walker's done very little to ingratiate himself in the short time I've been home, "You deserved it...shithead."

More sniggering. Walker flushes pink, furious I'm making an example of him, but he knows better than to speak again. No one else dares make a sound. Although satisfied my position as alpha male remains unchallenged by a week of absence, I'm flexing a little too bombastically. I've killed the usual atmosphere. I need to quit showing off and start getting back to normal.

I glance at my watch, "We're kinda late for this I'm guessing, but I heard in England any time is tea-time, right?"

Hope frowns in puzzlement.

"Tim, why don't you fetch the gift you got for Hope?"

Tim, the eldest and most clean-cut of the boys, bounces willingly to his feet and saunters to the shelves above the counter as the others nudge and whisper. He takes down a box wrapped in pink paper and tied with twine. As he carefully places it on the table before Hope, a reverent silence descends. It was Tim's thoughtful idea, texting me within hours of the ceremony to ask what they should buy, but they've apparently all contributed their dollars to the cost of this small welcome present for the new Mrs McCann.

I watch their faces and recall the conversations we've had at dinner over the last few weeks, the impending nuptials of such a confirmed bachelor as their over-the-hill boss a source of intense and sustained amusement. Collectively, they'd gleefully decided I was marrying Mrs Doubtfire: suitably old, frumpy, matronly, and about as far from the petite and enchanting reality seated at the opposite end of our kitchen table as it's possible to get. It's no wonder they've been struck dumb by the sight of her.

Hope glances uncertainly from the package to Tim's eager expression. Tim grins nervously and offers his pocket-knife, handle first, so she can slice the twine. A tentative smile lifts the corners of Hope's mouth at this boyish display of gallantry. Cautious fingers slide the blade from his open palm to gingerly cut the twist of cord. I'm holding my breath and feel foolish for doing so, but you could hear a pin drop in the expectant hush of the large room. One fingernail unpicks the tiniest edge of Scotch tape, peeling with torturous slowness. Spreading the gift wrap open with flat palms to reveal the box it contains, she slides deft fingers beneath the interleaved flaps, easing them upward and peering inside. I can hear the kitchen clock ticking. It's never been quiet enough in this goddam madhouse to hear it before. I find myself gazing distractedly up at it.

A noise from the opposite end of the table refocuses my attention. It's coming from Hope; a low giggle, bubbling in her mouth and escaping irrepressibly into the silent kitchen. Her little hands reach into the box and extract first a Union-Jack china teapot and then a matching mug, resplendent with a gleaming gold crown motif to either side. Clasping the mug against her chest, Hope's infectious grin widens until she's laughing with full-bodied, throaty satisfaction, green eyes shining at the bewitched boys ranged adoringly about her like worshipful knights before their Queen.

HOPE

Small-town America. My first experience of it. Mom and Pop stores, wide roads, traffic lights dangling on arched poles high above the carriageways. A crossing on each corner. Everything a straight line. No litter, no graffiti, the planters filled with attractive blooms, the grass mowed. Understated civic pride everywhere you look. It makes me ashamed to be English, with our inbred selfish disregard for anything beyond our own front door.

There are two lanes for traffic on either side of a sprawling central reservation, thereby making the near-deserted main street of this sleepy backwater town as broad as an English dual-carriageway. The buildings look as if a giant has come along with a flatiron to press them to their fullest extent. Long and low, unashamedly taking up space because they've got it in spades. Main street sports a hardware store, a mini-mart, a bar, a hairdresser, a steakhouse, a petrol station, a café bookshop and a bank, which I realise has no ATM.

I question Everett, "How do you get cash out?"

He grins, "Counter service. Go in and ask the Teller."

I gape, "No!"

"Welcome to 1950. Takes us a little while to catch up around here."

While he buys half the hardware store, I wander in a disbelieving daze from aisle to aisle, delighting in the crammed shelves. It has the homely feel of the 1980s shops of childhood. I note with glee that they keep the toilet brushes, sink plungers and shovels side by side, an illustrative tableau of how bad it could really get if you don't immediately deal with your blockage. I'm unable to suppress a snort of merriment at discovering they store the condoms adjacent to the retractable measuring tapes. The ultimate companion purchase. No pressure, cowboy.

Lugging his acquisitions out to the truck enables me to enjoy another very American phenomenon, the ability to park right outside where you want to go, for free. The English experience of parking half a mile away because that's the nearest space, paying an exorbitant fee for the privilege, and trudging a bad-tempered distance in chilly, persistent drizzle is clearly an annoyance firmly consigned to my past. Here, there are acres of spaces to choose from. Everett dumps the bags in the flatbed and shuts the lid, "Boot shop."

I feel immediate embarrassment. I haven't money for new shoes, and don't really know how to tell him, "It's not important…"

"You're in the Wild West now. Gotta look the part."

We wander back down the wide and empty pavement, Everett occasionally raising a hand to trucks rolling sedately by. I notice there's no one arguing, no one playing antisocially-loud music, no one speeding or jumping the lights, "It's very well-behaved here."

"As opposed to the hotbed of hedonism you've left behind?"

"I just mean the pace of life is slow."

"What's the hurry?"

We stop outside a long frontage. A middle-aged man with gleaming brogues is winding out the green and white striped sunshade, the ancient metal arms squealing as they extend their block of welcome shade.

"Everett!" I've noticed every greeting of my husband is a warm one. That must mean something. He knows a lot of people, and they all seem to like him.

"Hello, Earl. This is my wife, Hope. Hope, this is Earl of Earl's Boot Shop."

Earl shakes my hand enthusiastically and inclines his head quizzically at Everett, "I know good boots last years, but how come I never realised you were married?"

Everett winks, "Because I'm an international man of mystery, sir."

Earl raises a sardonic eyebrow, "Is that so, boy?"

"Sure is."

"What can I do for you?"

Earl opens the door of the shop for us. The interior is cool, dark and reeks of leather. The smell reminds me of the farmhouse tack room.

"Hope needs some new boots, and a hat that'll see her through a white and green season at least."

"Well, you've come to the right place. Giving the best service and the best quality since '74, Ma'am."

"You've been in business here since 1974?"

"That's right. Opened when my kids were young…and now I'm a great-grandpappy."

I scrutinise his face, thinking he's joking. His ebony features are virtually unlined, but the black hair is liberally dusted with grey at the temples.

"Don't you want to retire?"

"But why, child? I love the work I do. My business will endure as long as this community does. I've put shoes on the feet of every single person living here, and so I will for as long as the Good Lord allows."

"You must have seen a lot of change."

"Surprisingly little. When I was a boy, ranchers like Everett would ride a horse into town, or drive a cart. Now, they drive a truck, but they're still coming for the things that brought them seventy or more years ago…including a fine new pair of boots. You take a seat, child, and have a look there at all those racks of ladies' styles. What do you want them for, just riding? I'd say a stylish young lady like you needs a nice pair to wear out dancin' too – "

Everett stems the charming flow, "Hey! No selling me something impractical. She needs a decent pair of all-purpose riding boots. No fashion-crap, Earl!"

Earl winks at me and indicates a floor-to-ceiling rack crammed with every conceivable shape and style of what I would call a cowboy boot, but that no self-respecting cowboy would probably be seen dead in. Flat and wide through the foot, with a chunky block heel and leather loops to pull them on, they are a kaleidoscope of colours and designs. I glance uncertainly at Everett, "Which…?"

"Whatever you like the look of. Whatever fits nice."

Earl measures my feet on an old-fashioned sliding contraption I haven't seen since the shoe shops of childhood, "For your size, anything on this left-hand rack, my dear."

I stand before the shelves and look round at Everett, "I like all the ones with the colours and stitching."

"So, pick some."

I hesitate, "Will I get teased for having silly embroidered shoes?"

Everett inches up the leg of his jeans to reveal that the worn and weathered boots I'd assumed were tan leather are actually half teal-green, with gold and white stitching in two flared wing-shapes up the sides of the boot, resembling a soaring phoenix. Earl is quick to state, "Got those here."

Everett drops the leg of his jeans, and his boots revert to scuffed tan again. Smiling broadly, I select the pair that have been calling my name since we first walked in, leather so dark it's almost purple, resplendent with diamond-shapes of rainbow coloured stitching up the length of the leg; a little slice of sixties psychedelia in the sunbleached Wild West, "I love these."

"A great choice!" Earl's eyes light up – they must be the most expensive pair on the shelf – and he bustles through a beaded curtain into the stock room. Everett waits until Earl's out of sight before walking over and taking the display boot from me, examining the sole and taking heed of the handwritten price ticket. I waver, certain it says $200…but surely it can't, for shoes, in this tiny rural town?

"Are…are they…*expensive*?"

He shakes his head, "'Bout average. They'll last you a while, and you'll wear them for everything. A decent pair of well-made boots are worth the money. Earl's got all the patter but his stuff is good."

Now I'm worried. When do I confess that I can't actually buy them, that I'm wasting everybody's time?

Earl reemerges with the fabulous boots, unpacking them from their large box, folding back the layers of tissue paper and placing them on the carpet before me. They're tricky to wiggle on and I comprehend the need for the loops, hooking in my fingers and tugging hard.

"Tight through the foot, loose at the heel," Earl advises.

Once on, they feel made for me, with plenty of room to spread my toes, straight sides hugging my calves snugly. I walk about the shop and realise how slippery they are. I could almost skate across Earl's pristine bottle-green carpet.

"Whoa! Oh, they're too shiny!" At least that's a genuine reason for me not to have them. I feel relieved, and disappointed.

Earl looks troubled, sensing a sale slipping away, "You said you wanted them for riding…?"

Everett nods at him, "Hope, are they comfortable? Do they fit your foot properly? Do they rub at all?"

"No, they feel very cushiony and soft inside."

"Fitted to your foot, but not squeezing your toes?"

"They feel fine."

"Good. They're meant to be slippery. They don't have treads on the bottom."

"Why not?"

"So your foot slips easily out of the stirrup if anything happens. You don't run the risk of getting tangled up with the horse."

"Oh. Makes sense…"

"They'll rough up a bit over time anyway."

"Okay."

"Do you like them?"

Like them? I feel like the real thing: Annie Oakley, Calamity Jane, Daisy Duke, Dolly Parton. I can't stop myself strutting up and down, admiring my superb footwear in the low mirrors provided for the purpose.

"I *really* like them." Oh God, I need to shut up. I should say I'm not sure and I need to think about it. They need to go back in that box, safely under the tissue where I can no longer covet them.

"Everett, you heard the lady," Earl beams expansively and gathers up the packaging. He glances at my dusty, grubby trainers discarded on the carpet, "You want to wear your new boots now?"

I want to sleep in them, bathe in them, shimmy from coast to coast in them, but I can't. They have to go back. He grins, lifts my trainers in his fingertips before I can protest, and dumps them in the empty box with mild distaste. In Earl's opinion, there's clearly no excuse for shoddy footwear.

"Take the packaging, just in case. Wear them around for a few days. Any problems with fit or quality, bring them back."

"Oh, but – "

"Hat now," Everett steers me towards the forest of hat racks in the corner. Playing along until I can think of a face-saving way to avoid spending $200 I don't have, I gravitate towards the straw fedoras, the country-music-video parody of endless summer playing in my head. Everett is quick to tug me away, "No, no, no. The first downpour, those things become good for nothing but compost."

He points me towards the more practical hats, those you see everyone wearing. I try on one of dark cherry-brown, to match the rich colour of the tremendous boots. Everett smiles, "That's the one."

I beam, turn back to my reflection, feel the warmth of confidence surge in my chest. I'm too busy daydreaming to notice Everett walking away, but am brought clanging back to reality by the ring of the ancient cash register. Horrified, swinging around, whipping the hat off my head, I'm in time to see Everett passing over his credit card. Desperate, I skid across the smooth carpet in my unblemished boots.

"What are you doing?"

"What?" Everett's holding out his hand to take the boot box that now contains my rotten trainers, "You wearing your hat too?"

"But...but..." Everett smiles and takes my reaching, wavering hand.

"Let's go."

"But..."

Earl follows us to the door, beaming indulgently. As I stagger out into the street, blood rushing in my ringing ears, grasping the brim of the hat with clammy fingers, I hear him say to Everett, "I truly am getting old."

Everett clasps his shoulder, "Garbage, Earl! Evergreen!"

"No, I think this is the first time my faculties have failed me, boy. I don't remember you ever spending time in England, and I certainly never realised you were married. You'd have thought I'd recall that. How long ago did you two meet?"

Everett grins with irrepressible mirth, "How long ago? Oh, 'bout forty-eight hours, Earl. There ain't a darn thing wrong with your memory. Take care of yourself, now."

He slaps Earl good-naturedly on the shoulder, and we leave the old man gawping after us in frank bewilderment. Everett chuckles gleefully as he tosses the box into the truck's back seat, "That'll be all around town by lunchtime, but I don't care! I'm really starting to love what a conversation-stopper it is."

I'm out of breath, but I don't know why. Shock or shame? We need to talk about what just happened, but I'm struggling to form the right words. Had I given the impression I was assuming he'd pay? I grip the passenger door handle and stare at myself in the closest shop window.

Everett leans his elbows on the flatbed, "Admiring your new boots?"

"I was just thinking that doesn't look like me."

Everett points at the woman in the window, "Well, that's Mrs McCann."

"Who *is* she?"

Everett shrugs, "That's up to you to decide. Are you all right?"

"I don't know."

"Why not?"

"You paid, Everett. I didn't know you were going to do that. I hope you don't think I was assuming you would. I would never – "

"Happy Anniversary."

"What?"

"Well, a year is paper, or something. Two years is... I dunno. Twenty-five years is silver." He looks at his watch, "According to tradition, sixty-seven hours and thirty-two minutes is some new boots and a hat, right?"

EVERETT

She looks beautiful, my Wyoming wife. She's unfurling before me like a night-closed flower in the morning sun. She doesn't want to take off her new boots until I point out my officious sign on the tack room door, at which she laughs and complies.

At lunch, the boys are gratifyingly respectful of her, vying to be the first to make her laugh, pass the salt, cut her a slice of bread, fill up her water glass. Hope glows with delight at their well-meaning attentiveness, and asks endless questions about their lives and future intentions. She's enthusiastic, encouraging of confident declarations and the making of ambitious plans. They bask in the sunshine of her approval.

Once lunch is over, I take Hope to the corral to choose a good horse. Mo is fifty yards away, preparing the mounts he'll use for this afternoon's guest ride. I whistle, beckon him over.

"Boss? Ma'am." He tips his hat to Hope, who beams in response to his charming grin.

"I need your advice. What horse would be best for Hope to have, as a complete beginner?"

Mo stares ruminatively across the paddock at the grazing beasts, "Hmmm…not Julia. Too flighty."

"Which one's Julia?" Hope asks.

Mo points, "There. With the long mane."

He's indicating the handsome chestnut mare we've had from a foal, her long mane sweeping in an eye-catching coppery curtain much like Hope's own hair.

I agree, "Too skittish."

"Julia's a funny name for a horse."

"Julia Roberts. It's the long, red hair…"

Mo asks, "You taking Obi today?"

"I think so."

"Named after Obi-Wan-Kenobi?"

I laugh, whistle, and shout into the crowed of raised heads and blinking eyes, "Obi. C'mere Obi!" at full volume across the paddock. To Hope's evident amazement, Obi advances towards the fence like a well-trained hound, snorting a greeting and hanging his huge head over to get his ears rubbed. Hope takes several steps back, "He's massive!"

"Yeah, he's a big boy. Barack Obama."

"Why?"

"Because he's handsome and black with long legs."

Hope's giggling irrepressibly, "Are all your horses named after famous people?"

"Yep! Started off as a little joke between Jesse and I right at the beginning when we only had a few, but it's spiralled out of control over the years. We had the whole of the New Kids on the Block and the Jackson Five at one time, but they've either been sold on or are no longer with us. Only Donnie Wahlberg and Jermaine are left."

Her laughter is infecting Mo, who's chuckling away beside me as if he hasn't heard all this a hundred times before.

"See over there?" I point to a painted stallion, white with black patches around its eyes like a dairy cow, "that's Roy Orbison...and there," almost Roy's negative, a black painted with white patches to neck and eyes, "that's Ray Charles."

"Oh God," Hope groans, breathless with laughter.

"I think Mariah for Hope, don't you?"

Mo nods, still grinning, "Yeah. Placid, biddable..."

"Mariah?"

"Mariah Carey."

"I hesitate to ask...but why name a horse Mariah Carey?"

Mo chortles, "Because she whinnies a lot!"

Hope erupts again as a smiling Mo asks, "Shall I tack 'em up, Boss?"

"Please. We need to fit Hope to a saddle."

"Sure thing."

Mo returns to the corral to continue his preparations. Hope and I linger by the fence. Obi shakes his head happily as I scratch behind his ears. Hope's glance at Obi is wary, "Is Mariah as big as him?"

"No, Obi's an unusually big boy. She's a lot smaller."

"Good."

"She's a great girl. She's very calm, responds well to commands... She's used to being ridden by lots of different people, so she's not fussy or bad-tempered. She's super-patient, and if you like her, we'll keep her just for you to ride, and you can develop a nice bond with her. Like having any kind of pet, you find a way of communicating that transcends language."

"Okay. Um...I *am* nervous."

"I'll teach you the commands the horse understands, and we'll have a nice, slow, ambling ride so you can check out your new home. You'll be just fine. I will be with you every step of the way."

HOPE

True to their word, Mariah is a small, light brown mare with a glossy mane who stands uncomplainingly in the corral while Mo tacks her up, eating contentedly from a bucket hooked on the fence in front of her. Her back is above my head. She's nowhere near the monstrous size of Obi, but it still looks a long way to fall to me.

Everett swings himself onto Obi's high back and gives me the briefest of demos on how to stop, start and direct the horse, before leaping effortlessly down and strolling over to help me onto Mariah.

He stands behind me, loops the reins over the saddle horn, and holds the stirrup out for me, "Okay, Hope. Ball of the left foot in the stirrup."

I bend my leg up and slide the toe of my new boot cleanly into the wide loop of leather he holds still for me.

"With your left hand, grab a chunk of mane here, at the base of her neck. You won't hurt her. Right hand holds the back of the saddle. Bounce, bounce, and up you go."

I comply with these instructions and I'm sailing upwards with surprising ease and a poise I never usually possess. Mariah doesn't even move as I sink gently into the saddle and slide the toe of my new boot into the right-hand stirrup, suddenly appreciating the benefit of the slippery soles.

Everett pats my thigh, "Easy, huh? Now, rest the balls of your feet in the stirrups and push down with your heels. That action will keep you secure in the saddle. If you feel yourself rocking too much with the motion of the horse, just push your heels down."

"Okay."

Mariah decides something's not quite to her liking, and suddenly nods her head violently up and down. Petrified, I grip the saddle horn. Everett grins and prises my limpet fingers off the moulded leather pommel, "She's just having a fidget. Remember what I said, reins loose in your hand unless you're giving the horse an instruction. Then be gentle but firm, to give a clear signal what you'd like her to do. Otherwise, I want to see a loose, looped rein like a half-moon, so the bit doesn't pull on her mouth, okay?"

"Yes… Everett, what if she moves and I'm not ready?"

"Then give her an instruction. *You're* in charge of *her*, not the other way around."

"Okay." So far, to my intense relief, Mariah hasn't wanted to leave the contents of the bucket. Everett remounts Obi and turns him on a sixpence with enviable proficiency, "We're gonna go slow, steady, take our time and appreciate the scenery. I'll lead. Just tuck in behind me, but leave a few feet between us. Give the horses room around each other. Obi kicks if you get too close. He likes his personal space."

The idea of two massive, powerful animals engaging in fisticuffs I don't have the skill to manage brings my suppressed fear surging to the surface again, "Oh God, Everett. If he kicks her, what should I do?"

"Stop her. Stand still, and give the two of them some room. Hang back about five or six feet. That'll be perfect. He won't kick her anyway, I won't let him. Let's go. Remember how we get moving, a little jab of our heels in their side? Think loose rein, comfortable pace, push those heels down…and *relax*. These horses are used to being ridden. They know the trails well. This is routine stuff for them. Be calm and at one with your new pet."

Everett nudges the heels of his boots into Obi's vast body, "Let's go, Obi."

Heart pounding, breath short with nerves, I leave a space longer than I imagine Obi's kicking leg might be, then encourage Mariah to follow. She obeys with mellow willingness, walking sedately after Obi with a complaining snort as his kicked-up dust tickles her wide, pink nostrils. At first I'm convinced I'm just going to roll out of the saddle and crack my head on the stony track. I lurch from side to side with every step the horse takes. My rein is loose. I daren't clutch at it and antagonise the easygoing Mariah. I'm obviously not supposed to cling to the saddle horn. I tense my stomach muscles, clench my buttocks, and push down as hard as I can through my heels. Instantly, the rocking stops and I feel settled and solid. The motion of the horse beneath me is pleasant instead of terrifying, the clop of shoes on stones a soothing sound. Everett twists casually and rests a hand on the back of his saddle, asking, "Okay?"

"Don't you have to look where you're going?"

"Obi knows the way, don't you?" Everett reaches down and pats the rippling shoulder of the muscular horse.

We're moseying up the path marked private, towards the farmhouse.

"You're going on a trail no guests get to ride. We're going to go up behind the waterfall, the bit you can't see from the house. Gives you a great view of the whole ranch."

Nathan appears as we pass the farmhouse, mopping his way diligently out of the tack room door and stooping to upend the gush of dirty water into the dust outside. He catches sight of us and wiggles the mop in the air in response to my wave.

We cross the yard and take a narrow trail behind the farmhouse, in between the storage barns and the tumbledown 'gym', where the boys pump iron and pound the squeaking treadmill. Behind these barns, we're instantly into woods. One moment on a farm, the next in thick pine forest. The sudden silence and gloom are eerie. Even the thudding hooves of the horses are muffled by the dense carpet of fallen needles underfoot. The occasional bird call pierces the hush. The day is very still, the air hot and dry. I assume the horses must be grateful for the shade. We're climbing steadily on switchback trails that wind up the side of the steep pine-covered slope. Everett advises me to lean forward to help the horse. Here and there, little rocky streams cut through the vegetation, carving channels back down the hillside. They're each a maximum of three feet wide, but crossing the first is nevertheless a heart-stopping moment. There's a drop of several feet down the bank where I clench everything, push down through my heels as if my life depended on it, and lean back in my saddle like a limbo dancer. This is followed by several seconds of uncertainty as shod hooves negotiate stony riverbed. Then there's the steep clamber up a dusty bank on the other side, weaving between a cat's cradle of exposed tree roots, during which I lean forward with all my might. Once we've done a couple of these and I see Mariah is far more capable than I gave her credit for, I begin to feel like a real horse rider in my new boots and hat, secure in my wide saddle, leaning forward and back with the requirements of my mount and the demands of the trail, reins looped loose across my right palm, left hand dangling by my thigh like a carefree cowgirl. It's then that I begin to relax and enjoy the ride. Mariah's surefooted steadiness and calm demeanour mean my input is minimal. She's simply following along behind Obi as if we're a desert camel-train. Everett periodically glances behind to check on me, but seems largely satisfied to let me ride unsupervised, which must mean I'm managing okay. He occasionally points out some interesting piece of flora or fauna, once spotting two deer drinking from a tributary of the stream we've just crossed, putting a finger to his lips and pointing them out as we meander unobtrusively past. The horses slow now and again to tear at the undergrowth bordering the trail, chewing and snorting with satisfaction.

As we ascend further, the tree cover thins considerably. We're suddenly out of the forest's dappled shade and into the full afternoon sun once more, on trails of loose dust that kicks up around us and makes me squint and pull my hat brim down to protect my eyes. Mariah snorts irritably and does two big sneezes, as if to reproach Obi for the cloud he's created. The path in front of us looks so steep I'm sure I'd have to crawl up it on hands and knees if we were walking. However, I now have every confidence in Mariah, and lean forward as far as I can to take the weight off her back and help her balance. She pants breathily in the thin, dry air of our high-altitude location, emerging onto the rocky plateau behind Obi expelling several triumphant farts at having made it without incident. Everett is waiting for me rather too near the edge of the promontory of overhanging rock at the very top of the slope. I stop Mariah about fifteen feet away, "That's as close as I dare to get."

He grins, turns the horse and comes back to me, pointing behind us, "There you go. That's home."

I turn my head and am stunned to see the ranch sprawling below us like the view from an aeroplane window. The huge buildings are the size of shoeboxes, the trucks like children's toys on a play farm. I knew we'd been progressing steadily uphill, but the twists of the trail belied the steepness of the climb.

"How high up are we?"

Everett shrugs, "Nine thousand feet, maybe?"

"Wow! The ranch looks so tiny!"

I fumble my 'phone from my pocket and snap a picture or two. The ranch, my smiling husband on his glossy black horse, a mini-movie of the panorama before me, "Incredible…"

I hold out my 'phone to Everett, "Will you take a picture of me with Mariah?"

"Sure." He leads Obi away a few feet and snaps a shot. He hands back the 'phone, "Just had to make sure I got the boots in…"

I roll my eyes at the teasing and gaze back down at the ranch once more.

"This morning when you woke up, did you ever believe you'd have ridden your new horse to nine thousand feet by dinner time?"

I shake my head, beaming delightedly.

"And so competently, too."

I glow with a pride I'm unable to conceal.

"Now, we're going down the other side of this outcrop and onto that prairie you can see, then back across the river and up the side of the ridge to the corral again."

"How deep is the river?"

"Oh, not deep. Just over the knee."

"The *knee*? What about my *boots*?"

Everett chuckles, "The *horse's* knee, Hope."

"Oh… Oh yeah…of course…"

Everett limbos in the saddle, "Remember, going downhill, *leeeean baaaack*."

I laugh, "Got it."

"Still pushing down through those heels?"

"Still pushing!"

"Good girl. Let's go."

Downhill, although trickier to balance, is more rewarding for the novice rider. I feel positively professional as I lean as far back in the saddle as I'm able, experiencing the satisfying stretch of my stomach muscles, squeezing my buttocks and enjoying the tension in my thighs as my heels thrust down and my calves stretch. It's no wonder everyone here has such an impressive physique. This is a full-body workout with added scenery. Replaying the upward route in my mind, I suddenly realise what we've done, "Everett, did we cross above the waterfall?"

"Yeah. We climbed up to that bare area above the trees that you can only just see from the farmhouse. Now, we're dropping down to the prairie, and we'll cross back over the river by Jesse and Mel's."

"Is this your land?"

"No, Ma'am. The river is our boundary. This here is public land. Anyone can roam these trails."

I glance left and right, "Is there even anyone else *here*?"

He laughs, "There's other folks around. We're just not living one on top of the other like I think people do where you come from."

"I've never been anywhere before where you can't see at least one other house, or hear a road or an aeroplane."

Everett wrinkles his nose, "I'd hate that."

"It's not great," I acknowledge, "This is better."

The tree cover is thinning, the path levelling out. Tall meadow grass and delicate wildflowers predominate here, rather than the rosehip, raspberry and choke-cherry bushes of the higher trails. Everett stops Obi and holds up a palm to stay me too, beckoning me slowly forward, indicating I should be quiet.

"What?"

"Look." The prairie grass is so tall that at first I can't see what he's pointing at, then the large, brown shape I'd assumed was a rock begins to move with a slow, lumbering gait, and I notice there are more moving boulders beside it.

"What's that?"

"Buffalo. Imagine coming across that prairie with no idea what you'd find over the next hill, no map to speak of, rumours flying about the whereabouts of raiding bands of natives who want your cattle or your horses, no clue where the next water source is, no information on whether the rivers you're due to cross will be passable or not...and then you encounter a herd of a few hundred of those, and they can run at forty miles an hour! I don't necessarily agree with much of what the incomers did in the Old West, but you've gotta admit they were intrepid people."

"Or what they were coming from was *so* bad that what they were going to had to be better, stampeding buffalo or not."

It strikes me I'm on my own pioneering odyssey, and anticipating no less bounteous results than the first incomers to cross this epic landscape. We watch the grazing beasts for several minutes, the patient horses swishing their tails and munching the grass and flowers with every bit as much relish as their bovine neighbours.

"If they stick around this area for the winter, you might see some babies come the springtime."

"What are the babies like?"

"Like super-hairy calves. They're very cute. They run around and jump like all little animals do. They're great to watch. Tim has pictures of some baby ones from a couple of years ago. He made them into postcards for the hotel."

As the small buffalo herd moves away, Everett leads us out of the sparse tree cover and onto the open prairie, turning us right towards the hotel. It looks impressive, perched on the high ridge above the ravine.

"I hope that picture's in the brochure." I take out my 'phone and snap a couple of shots.

"Sure is…"

Everett looks across at me. We're moving together through the long grass, ten feet apart, the strong legs of the horses disturbing crackling crickets, fluttering insects and puffs of wildflower pollen.

"Want to try cantering?"

I bite my lip, "I don't know…do I?"

"Yes. We won't go fast. We'll canter these few yards to the river, slow the horses, cross the water, yeah?"

"Okay… How do I do it?"

"Just dig in your heels to get her moving, and keep digging them in until she's going at the speed you want. If she gets too fast, check her with the reins. Ready?"

"As I'll ever be."

"Okay, get her moving, and we'll keep pace with you."

I push my heels into Mariah's sides and she walks faster. Another couple of digs and she picks up her feet, taking dainty, prancing strides through the long grass, bouncing me crazily in the saddle until I regain the presence of mind to push down my heels and steady myself. After that, instead of my teeth clacking sharply together and my boobs bouncing painfully, I realise the firmness through my thighs is holding me slightly above the saddle and enabling me to move with fluidity, matching the rhythm of the horse. I'm even brave enough to urge her faster still, but my new-found courage fails me as I catch sight of the river. I slow Mariah way too early and am back to our pedestrian amble twenty yards before I need to be. Everett, still alongside, glances questioningly at me. I nod towards the river, "Lost my bottle a bit."

He smiles and looks at his watch, "Your total time on a horse is just over three hours. Mine is almost thirty-eight years. You are doing *fantastically*."

We're at the river. It's clear and shallow – I can see the rocks on the bottom – but the current is swift. A few trails of weed skim past us, tumbling and turning in the fast water.

Everett's watching me, "Take it slow. Let Mariah find her own way across."

I encourage Mariah to follow Obi. She takes tentative steps onto the uneven, wet pebbles, shod hooves occasionally slipping on the stones. Each time she does this, my heart is in my mouth, but we ford the river without incident – even stopping mid-passage for a drink – and she's as sure-footed emerging from the water as she's been for the whole ride.

After that, it's a doddle. A gentle meander down the river bank past the bottom of Jesse and Mel's garden, up the well-travelled trekking trail to a woodland clearing where there's evidence of a recent campfire in the centre of a circle of logs, and through the winding forest trail to emerge back at the corral. As we get closer to home, Mariah starts to whinny and toss her head.

"Is she okay?"

"She's excited. She knows she's gonna get food when she gets back."

"What should I do?"

"Let her do her thang. She's just going, 'Oats, lovely oats!'"

"What treats can you give a horse?"

"Carrots, apples... They like mints, sugar lumps... Walker accidentally gave Michael Jackson a cough lozenge once. He only realised it wasn't a toffee once he'd given it to him. He said Michael did two laps of the corral with his tail up and his nostrils flaring, then came back and tried to get another one!"

This makes me squawk with laughter, attracting Mo's attention as we thump back over the hard earth and through the gate into the corral. He's already taking the saddles off the guest horses he'd been tacking up as we left. Everett dismounts and tethers Obi to the fence. Mo comes over and takes my reins from me, "You two were ages! I've been back a half hour already."

"We went right up to the overhang. Came back down onto the prairie. Saw a few buffalo down there."

"Oh yeah? Enjoy it?" Mo asks me.

"Loved it."

"How'd she get on?"

Everett smiles proudly, "A natural."

"Great!"

They look expectantly up at me.

"How do I get off?"

Everett grins, "Right foot out of the stirrup. Right hand on the back of the saddle, left hand on the front, swing your leg over the horse's back and stomach on the saddle as you ease yourself down."

I manage an approximation of his instructions and end up on two feet with solid ground underneath me, turning to my chuckling audience and admitting, "Not as graceful as on the way up."

I pat Mariah affectionately on the neck. Her big, brown eyes regard me steadily, long lashes blinking. It's impossible to tell if she likes me or not. Mo leads her away for water, food and a well-earned brush, untying Obi as he passes and leading the two horses side by side towards the corral tack room. Walker emerges from its gloom to help him.

"Could you get on with riding Mariah?" Everett asks me.

"Yes, she's very forgiving."

"You didn't put a foot wrong today."

"I feel a bit guilty just going off and leaving them to sort out my horse. Shouldn't I be helping?"

"No, you're the boss's wife, and it's their job. Plenty of time to learn how to do it all another day. You can go out on her whenever you like. Tag on the back of the groups the boys take out, learn the trails, get used to Mariah and let her get used to you. Then you've got the freedom to roam wherever you choose."

"I like the idea of that. It seems impossible I'll ever be that accomplished."

"A year from now, you won't be able to remember a time when you couldn't do it."

I stand on tiptoe to kiss his cheek, "Thank you."

"For what?"

"For opening my eyes."

Everett beams and sweeps me along in the crook of his huge arm, "Come on. Let's go have a coffee and unpack the bags we've been ignoring since yesterday. We need to find a home for all your things. Then you need to brace yourself for one of Nathan's dinners."

"*Brace* myself?"

"It's what those food journos call a 'culinary sensation'…just not in a good way. However, he's learning, and everyone takes their turn, so you have to mentally hold your nose and get it down without it touching the sides."

I grimace, "Why doesn't someone just teach him to cook?"

Everett sniggers, "What makes you think the rest of us are any better?"

We're laughing easily together as we bundle into the tack room, skittering trails of dust from the toes of our boots onto the freshly-mopped floor.

****

This house usually clatters, bangs, thuds, squawks, creaks, hoots and buzzes with industry, conversation, bustle and banter. Now, at eleven in the morning, it's silent as the grave. The slap of my flip-flops echoes on the tiles as I wander down the corridor to the kitchen. Standing in the doorway, at first I'm only aware of the ticking of the clock. Then, I hear the intrusive whirr of the camera motor, detecting my movement and turning its hateful lens upon me. Unable to prevent myself, I glare murderously at it, as if my animosity will make it avert its big, black eye…but all I'm doing is glaring at any viewers we might have like a lunatic old shrew. I need to find something better to do than obsess about the cameras. I've unpacked all my things over the last couple of days, in between spending some very relaxed and pleasurable time with my new husband: walking, horse riding, chatting endlessly about anything and everything. He talks with animation about raising his brother, describing their abject poverty with touching candour. Despite his many self-deprecating denials, it's obvious whose tireless toil is responsible for the stratospheric success of Ralton Parker's adult life. It explains why he looked at Everett with worshipful adoration when we arrived unannounced on their doorstep, and why Everett gazed back with such paternal pride. He's now expending that same effort with all the desperate lads who wind up at Ridge River, their last-chance saloon. I swiftly comprehend that where Jesse Cole is the stick, my mellow husband is the carrot. Jesse appears infrequently and puts the fear of God into them with his well-honed ice-man act, implying he expects nothing less than total obedience, and not an inch of backsliding. By contrast, Everett ensures loyalty and good behaviour by assuming rather than demanding it. He commends endeavour, regardless of success, and they learn not to give up. They strive to earn and retain Everett's trust, desperate for his notice and praise. It's more than simply impressing your boss. It's greater even than hero-worship. It's nothing less than love for him. They joke at his expense, tease him as much as they dare, imply he's old and uncool, call him 'Dad'…but it's because they wish he was. Everett is quick to enforce discipline and control, but he's quicker to smile, to encourage, and to hug. He tells me some of them have never been held in their lives until arriving here, before enveloping me in his big arms and declaring, "and everybody needs a cuddle now and again, right?"

Just *being* at Ridge River is to experience the affectionate gathering within a secure and tight embrace of inclusion, acceptance and solidarity. It pulls everybody towards the centre of this world, gently revolving with the rhythm of the days, the pattern of the seasons, and the routine of the tasks they generate. It's heart-breaking that such a wonderful, willing father figure, with a proven record of raising and repairing other people's damaged offspring, will never have a child of his own. It doesn't seem fair. I feel the same sharp sting of emotion I used to experience when impotently raging against the uselessness of my own body. I bury the sensation swiftly. I've got better at that over the years. In my twenties, I'd wait until I was alone in the house and then throw plates at the kitchen wall. The excessive anger would eventually abate, and I'd be left sweeping up smashed crockery and having to buy a new set. I only ever threw the cheap stuff, but it was still a ridiculous way for a grown woman to behave. By my thirties, I'd developed the skill of rolling the anger into a tight little internal ball, swallowing it down into the pit of my stomach, where it sat like a cloth-covered cheese left to mature, bound and festering. I'm shocked to taste its bitter bile in my throat again. I make myself a cup of tea to take away the familiar tang of failure. I feel better as I stand by the boiling kettle and look down at my new mug. Strangers thought about me. Strangers bought me a present because they knew that, shortly, I wouldn't be a stranger any more. I make my tea, resolutely keep my face turned away from the two cameras in the massive room, and wander back down the corridor to my new apartment.

I mooch absently along the wall of untidily-crammed bookshelves. Everett doesn't own a television. There's one in the kitchen where the sofas are, but the boys commandeer the remote and argue ceaselessly about what to watch, or fall asleep in front of DVDs of endless car chases and shoot-outs. Slim chance of me being able to watch one of my own English tv boxsets, brought from home for purely-nostalgic reasons. Everett is a voracious reader and, judging by the bookshelves, a discerning consumer of reasonably highbrow literature. There's as much non-fiction and biography on the shelf as there are thrillers, westerns and classics. He reads science, history, politics, philosophy, religion, ethics, travel, and yet told me he'd barely been to school. I've got seven-eighths of a degree and I've never read the kind of weighty tome favoured by my uneducated husband. Forget the boxsets, I need to start improving my bibliography!

I twirl listlessly on the wooden floor, eyes glazing. Not even lunchtime. The first day without Everett babysitting me and I have no idea how to amuse myself. I think back. Before I had that crummy office job, how did

I fill my days? Recalling that shallow time makes me cringe with shame. I suppose I used to tidy up, do housework, prepare meals…? I can't do that now. I can organise our own house, which I've done this morning, but the rest of the place is a team effort. Although responsible for keeping their own rooms tidy, the task of cooking and maintaining the cleanliness of the communal areas is shared on a rolling rota. Everyone takes their turn, including Everett. I will be expected to do my share. I notice my name has already appeared on the whiteboard. No one gets a free ride here, but the roster means no one gets stuck being the eternal floor-mopper or potato-peeler either. Clever old Everett. The more I learn about him, the more I admire him. Apparently, Mo's cooking is best and Nathan's worst…but they eat it, because they're ravenous, and because that's how they roll. Here, they say, 'Be sure to taste your words before you spit 'em out.' It's sage advice. If you dish it out, you've got to be able to take it, too.

Besides the daily grind of the housework, how else did I amuse my vacuous former self? I used to snack…a lot. Occasionally ring my mother. Meet my so-called friends for shopping, coffee and recreational bitching about whichever of our social circle was absent and therefore fair game. God, I was a vile excuse for a human being! I must make a supreme effort never to be like that *ever* again. No one knows me in America. My pathetic past is over six thousand miles away. I've got the luxury of a blank canvas. I need to ensure I'm proud of what I paint upon it from now on.

My restless feet come to a stop before the fireplace. There are a few photographs on the mantlepiece I haven't had a chance to take a close look at yet. One is a posed studio shot of Ralton's brood. It's a cute, middle-class family portrait in an expensive-looking frame. 'We love you, Uncle Everett' is written in one corner in a childish, rounded hand.

Next to it is a superb picture that makes me crow aloud at the sight of it. A young Everett, thick sideburns halfway down his cheeks, twinkle-eyed grin, foot up on a haybale next to an enormous cup. He wears huge and ostentatious chaps complete with more fringe than a Beatles tribute band, emblazoned with sponsors logos as copiously as any billboard. A gigantic silver buckle is on his jeans, his thumbs are hooked casually into his pockets, his chin is lofted, and his blue eyes glint with steely defiance at the photographer's lens. He manages to look both adorable and arrogant at the same time. I read the plaque propped against the bale. I don't understand most of it – sponsors names and jargon – but it's quite clear he's champion of something. The year is 1995. He's twenty-six. He told me the decade between twenty-five and thirty-five was the golden time – big money, dizzying success – so this must be the start of it all, a young man on the cusp of greatness. It's a wonderful picture: cheeky, cheesy, confident and charismatic. Very American. You may scoff at us, world, but look at how darn *well* we're doing…

In the centre of the mantlepiece, there's a small, square frame containing a photograph so faded and battered I can't make it out at first. I take it down, carry it to the window, scrutinise it in the bright daylight. A young woman with long brown hair and a flowery dress sits cross-legged and barefoot in a field of faces. On her lap is a very grubby, chubby, happy baby. The young woman has butterflies painted on her cheeks, a daisy-chain around her head, and she's laughing as heartily as the child. Beside her sits a blonde, bare-chested man with filthy bare feet, who wears a wide-brimmed brown hat from beneath which his long hair protrudes. His big hand holds the baby's tiny one. Although his face is turned from the camera, my first thought is that this is Everett. The attitude is identical, the shape of the jaw the same, the build comparable. Is this a secret child he hasn't yet seen fit to reveal? But surely it can't be Everett? The picture is old. The style of clothing, the size and appearance of the photograph, its faded condition; everything about it suggests the sixties. I peer closely at the woman's face. I've seen it before. A moment's consideration and I return to the mantlepiece, holding the picture up beside Ralton's family portrait. The faces are the same. The woman with the long hair has Ralton's pointed chin, Ralton's soulful brown eyes, Ralton's chestnut hair. This smiling young girl is their dead mother. The man I assumed must be Everett is the father he can't remember, and the fat, happy baby is my husband. Potentially, this precious, preserved picture from five decades ago is the only family portrait Everett will ever have. Its presence next to the casually-posed shot of Ralton's family – presumably one photograph amongst hundreds they possess – makes it all the more poignant. Everett's family is the past. Ralton's is the future. Who sacrificed every chance of his own to give his brother that future but Everett himself? A lump comes to my throat and I fumble the priceless keepsake back onto the mantlepiece.

The final photograph also looks old, but not as battered as Everett's baby picture. I take it down and look at it. Recognisably, Everett grins with characteristic cheeky charm, swinging a little boy high in his arms towards the camera. At first I assume it's his nephew, Ryan, but the Everett in the picture looks a teenager. The boy in the photograph must be Ralton, one tiny trainer flying off his foot and up into the air. As Everett swings him, he's laughing his little head off. I wonder who took the picture. The landscape behind is bare and arid, but a few horses are visible, grazing the distant scrub. I turn the picture over and carefully remove the back of the frame, wondering if Everett does the same thing as my mother and writes on the back of his photographs. Sure enough, in spidery scrawl, it says, 'Ray's Ranch, '83: teaching Ralton to tie his shoes.'

1983. I work it out. Everett was fifteen, and Ralton only five. The test of his baby brother's shoe-tying ability was clearly a rigorous one, judging by the height he's chucking Ralton and the exhilarated delight on the little boy's face. Can I ask who Ray is? If I do, he'll know I've been snooping at his pictures. Both boys look thin, and there's a discernible row of suspicious black bruises down Everett's right arm, close to the camera as he throws Ralton.

Something niggles at me. That precious fifty-year-old picture he's held onto through every trial and struggle. His family. Where he comes from. It's okay for Ralton. Where he comes from is defined by Everett. He has a past, an anchor for his beliefs and traditions. It's his brother, from five-year-old shoe-tying to the University graduation picture I saw in Melanie's album. What does Everett have to root him? A battered photograph of the back of his father's head, and a long-dead mother.

He'll openly talk about his twenties and the two brothers struggling to get by; his thirties, and the success he finally enjoyed, the little slice of showbiz that paid for all this; the hard graft of his forties, building this place into a success – but barely anything about his childhood. From that beaming, dirty baby to the cheeky, swaggering champ in his chaps and buckles, there's a yawning chasm of mystery he won't allude to. If I try a question or two, he changes the subject. Why? Something to do with his Mum's nasty boyfriend and the scar across his face? I want to know, but I don't want to deliver pain by asking.

I'm startled from my reverie by the clatter of a bucket on the hallway tiles. I peek out of the door and there is Hedge, mopping like a demon because he wants to go to town this afternoon, and Jesse has promised to take him only if all his chores are done.

"Hey, Leyton." I feel I don't know him well enough for the nickname.

He stops, looks petrified for a millisecond, then stands erect like a sentry, mop by his side, tugging his forelock like a serf saluting his lady, "Ma'am."

"Want a hand with anything?"

He looks positively panicked at the suggestion, "It's not your day, Ma'am…it's my day…"

He gestures helplessly towards the kitchen, the whiteboard, the rota. I release him from his anxious confusion, "No problem. I thought I might go outside. Shall I go now so I don't walk on your clean floor?"

He beams, "Yes, please, Ma'am."

"Okay. Hang on, just let me get some socks."

I sprint upstairs for a pair, grab my 'phone and scuttle past him, "Thanks, Leyton. See you later."

"Bye, Ma'am." He stands to attention, watching me until I'm right down the opposite end of the corridor, then resumes his frenetic mopping.

I go out into the tack room, sit on a bench, put on my socks, tug on my tremendous boots with a tingle of excitement. I take my hat off my hook and put it on. I instantly feel like I did when I stared at my unfamiliar reflection in the downtown shop window. I'm in disguise as a woman who knows what she's doing, and what her life's all about. She knows where she's going and why she's travelling there. I've no idea what I'm going to do in the farmyard any more than I knew what to do indoors, but I'm determined to find something. It's my intention to get out there, fit in, and make myself useful.

Outside, the first thing I'm aware of is the high camera on the pole affixed to the end of the nearest barn, able to take in the whole yard. There's another that overlooks the corral too. Why is it wherever I go in this beautiful place, the first thing I notice is the presence of the damned camera, instead of pleasant hot sun, warm breeze on my skin, the satisfying crunch and grind of the stony earth under my boots, the scent of the pines, the rush of the waterfall? They're going to be here for twelve months. I've publicly declared I'm okay with that. I've signed a legal document to that effect. I need to get on with it. Currently, their behaviour controls mine. Old Hope Howarth might have allowed this to endure indefinitely. New Hope McCann will *not*. I must be so busy and involved in my new life that I don't have time to care whether it's being recorded or not.

How to do this? What to choose to occupy myself? With determination, I crunch off optimistically up the path to the cowsheds, pastures and cultivated fields, sure I'll find something. The first people I encounter are Tim and Nathan, engaged in what looks like a fairly comprehensive service of a large piece of farm machinery. There are components lined up on an old grease-stained towel, and both are serious, quiet, absorbed in methodically working through their task. A radio plays faintly somewhere. Tim glances up as I cast a shadow, "Good morning."

"Hello. That looks very involved."

"Bit of maintenance… Harvest soon."

"Ah, I see."

"What are *you* up to?" Tim seems glad of the break, easing from his crouching position to wander over to me. Nathan doesn't even notice I'm there, so engrossed is he in following the path of a wire up to a junction box.

Tim inclines his head towards him, "We've got an electrical problem."

I whisper, "He's sixteen, Tim. Can he fix it?"

He nods without hesitation, "Oh yeah…he's an engineer in the making."

I smile, "I won't keep you. I want to be useful, but I'm no use in here!"

Tim grins, wiping his greasy hands on a rag, "Well, it sure was kind of you to drop by."

"Good luck with it…"

"Thanks. I've got every faith in him."

As he speaks, Nathan grunts and flicks out the broken end of a wire. Tim bounds over to him, "Got it?"

"Uh-huh," Nathan waggles the frayed copper with his screwdriver.

Tim claps him on the back, "Nice!"

Nathan grins smugly. Tim chortles, "You've just gotta strip it out and replace it now!"

Nathan pulls a face and hunches over the box again, deft fingers working busily. Tim glances across and gives me a thumbs-up. I smile, wave, and leave them to it.

Up at the cowsheds, I can hear the splashing of water against concrete. I peek around the huge roller-door. It's the milking parlour. The ranch keeps a small dairy herd for the requirements of hotel and home. Walker's there in overalls and wellingtons, sluicing down the parlour from morning milking. I don't want to engage with him. I decide to carry on, quickly, but he's already spotted me. He smirks nastily, and drawls, "Keeping tabs, Mommy?"

I'm determined not to let him get under my skin, forcing a smile and trilling with false gaiety, "Just out for a walk!"

I take a couple of steps into the parlour and he twitches the hose towards me. I'm not sure if the action is playful or spiteful, but it makes me shuffle hastily backwards across the concrete, protecting my precious boots. Irritation pricks me. Who does this little oik think he is? I scowl, examining my boots for signs of damage, but when I look up expecting to see him grinning at my discomfiture, his expression is open, "Don't walk in here in those! You'll wreck 'em!" I notice his big eyes are such a light hazel they seem golden in the sunlight shining through the parlour door. I decide to try a different approach than I've previously employed in my so-far-unsuccessful interactions with him, "Can I help you with anything?"

He gapes in unconcealed amazement, "You *are* kidding, right?"

"Um…no? I was at a loose end, so I wondered if I could make myself useful."

He laughs loudly, rudely, "Listen, lady, I don't know how y'all do things in England, but if Everett McCann catches me letting you sluice cowshit out of the parlour in your best new booties, we'll be eating my roasted junk for lunch! You get me?"

I'm not sure what gives me the confidence to do it, possibly his allusion to my superb footwear, but I extend a leg and rotate my ankle before him, "Do you like them?"

He sniggers and I await a derisive comment, but instead he grins and admits, "Yeah. They're nice. I've got a pair a bit like that for competing."

"Oh. You'll have to show me sometime. What do you compete as?"

"Saddle bronc rider."

"What's that?"

"Bucking horse?"

"Oh, right…I've seen pictures of that. Looks dangerous!"

He shrugs, wanting to boast, knowing he can't, "I guess…"

"Do you do well?"

"I've won some money before now…"

"Wow!" I pretend to be much more impressed than I actually am, pleased we've finally been able to have a halfway civil conversation. He releases the gun of the hose and the powerful gush ceases instantly. It suddenly feels very quiet and a bit too private up here, as Walker prowls towards me, wellingtons schlopping on the wet floor. The image of young Everett in his chaps from the mantlepiece photograph springs to mind. It's something about the look on Walker's face, "At a loose end, huh?"

Confused, I'm definitely frightened of him, but he's undeniably attractive in an edgy, dangerous kind of way. Increasingly flustered the closer he gets, I breathe, "What does your girlfriend think about you doing these hazardous sports?"

He stops short, really thinks about it, murmurs wonderingly, "Do you know, she's never said…"

"She must approve then, or she wouldn't stop going on about it. That's women for you!"

"She likes it when I win money. Most of it goes on her goddam college books!"

"When she's qualified, she'll be a well-paid woman."

He snorts a laugh, "Here's hopin'!"

"You must miss her."

A gentle expression washes across his hard features. His eyes look into mine, but it's not my face they see, "Yeah, but she's back Friday…and she needs to stay close with her folks. You don't toss a life like that down the shitter for no good reason but stupid pride."

"She's got her principles…?" I bait, understanding there's been a bit of a rift between Rosemary and her wealthy family over her choice of career, home and boyfriend.

Walker sniggers sarcastically and dangles the gun of the hose down onto the toe of his boot, nudging it absently and making it swing. Water dribbles out of the end and across the yellow toe of his wellington, "You can't climb a mountain with your legs roped together, know what I'm saying?"

It's a great analogy, and makes me laugh aloud.

"I'm really looking forward to meeting her."

"You are? Why?"

"She must be a formidable girl to keep control of you."

His grin is wide with genuine amusement, shrugging with rogueish innocence, protesting, "Me? I'm a pussycat!"

"More like a tiger."

He growls at me, snaps the hose on again, and swaggers back into the parlour without a backward glance.

I sigh, shake my head, press on towards the fields, chuckling quietly. Perhaps he isn't as bad as I first thought?

I walk out onto the stony lanes that run between the fields, wide trails down which they drive everything from machinery to livestock. The grazing cows low with insistent, loud regularity, though whether warning each other of my presence or simply making conversation, I'm not qualified to tell. I detect a building, chugging roar behind me, and scuttle rapidly to the safety of the fence as Jesse bears down upon me behind the wheel of a tractor. As he passes, he waves enthusiastically, smiling wide. I wave and smile back, but have to turn swiftly and shield my eyes with the brim of my hat as the dust cloud engulfs me. It's harsh and drying in my mouth, making me moisten my lips and run my tongue along my teeth to dispel the gritty sensation. Once the tractor has passed I'm alone once more, with only the distant rush of the waterfall, the sharp crackle of the crickets, and the lowing of the cows. There's no one around up here, and therefore nothing I can to do be useful.

I turn and retrace my steps, reentering the yard at its opposite corner to avoid another encounter with the disconcerting Walker. I find Mo in the stables, forking manure into a large wheelbarrow with practised proficiency.

"Hello, Mo."

"Good morning, Ma'am."

He smiles, he's polite, but he doesn't stop bending, pushing, straightening, flicking...

"Can I help you with anything?"

His reaction is more measured than Walker's, but equally emphatic, "That's very kind of you, Ma'am, but we can't have you pitchforking manure, can we? What would the boss say?"

I put my head on one side and coyly enquire, "What *would* the boss say, Mo?"

"He'd probably ask to borrow my fork and then chase me out of town with it!"

I laugh, "So I definitely can't help you then?"

He shakes his head, "Not if I don't want extra holes in my ass! You're very kind, but I'm good. I have a little rhythm going here."

I nod, "Very efficient."

He smiles, "See you at lunch."

"Okay."

Rebuffed again, albeit gently, I trudge disconsolately back up the private track from corral to farmyard, quite at a loss what to do with myself. I pause at the edge of the wood, staring out across the yard, feeling like a spare part. Suddenly, I spot Everett and Alex. They're standing before the bull pens, backs to me. I like Bo and Luke, the two huge bulls. Bo is dappled white with a mussy coat, hairy brown ears he flaps endearingly, and a long brown tail that whips and waves as enthusiastically as any dog's. He's tame enough to come up to the fence and take a beetroot from your outstretched palm. By contrast, Luke is glossy black, sleek all over, rippling with solid muscle. He grunts, snorts, bucks his fearsome head and looks permanently furious. Only Jesse and Everett dare to venture into Luke's pen.

Encouraged by the sight of Everett, I'm confident enough to step from the tree cover and stride briskly towards them. The closer I get, the clearer it becomes that they are in deep discussion, and I feel pathetic for interrupting and hanging around just because I'm bored and lonely. I change direction, trying to make it look as if I was heading for the farmhouse all along. Alex is the first to notice me, nodding and raising a hand to the brim of his hat. I haven't yet seen him smile in the short while I've been here. He's not unpleasant or nasty, but he's also neither talkative nor approachable. He and Everett are arguing over the pages of a diary, and don't immediately notice me. The large book is propped on the fence in front of them, and Bo observes them closely from the opposite side, as if participating in the discussion. There's a lot of flicking through the pages and animated gesticulation. Everett glances at Alex for his opinion, and looks around to see what's caught the young vet's eye. An expression of such delight settles on his face that for a moment my body quite forgets how to walk and I stumble and trip in my slippery soles in the stony dust, blushing and fidgeting. It's been so long since anyone's reacted to the sight of me with such obvious pleasure. I wave as nonchalantly as I can manage in my halting progress back to the house. Occasionally, I glance behind me. Alex's attention has returned to the diary, but Everett's intense gaze follows me every step of the way.

EVERETT

Alex is driving me crazy. He's suddenly insisting that some random stock vaccination must happen in the middle of harvest, and can't seem to understand everyone else's inability to be in two places at once. We're going around in circles because he's refusing to listen, and then Hope walks across the yard and my mind empties of everything but her. I can't even remember why I was getting so annoyed. All I can think is that this is bullshit; an argument I can't win because I'm talking to someone who obstinately refuses to see reason, and a wife I can't make love to in my own home because there are cameras all over it that freak her out.

I watch Hope's passage across the yard, her beguiling body clad in t-shirt and jeans, an outfit all the more attractive for its simplicity. She's not trying, she's just beautiful. Her copper hair shines in the sunlight. I suddenly have something more important to do than bicker.

Hedge is mopping his way across the tack room when I open the door and rush inside. In the gloom, I don't spot him until he nearly backs into me, "Whoa!"

"Oh! Sorry..."

"It's okay... Look, just let me get my boots off..."

I hop around crazily, trying to lever off my boots at speed, spreading mud on the bit he's already mopped, "Sorry, Hedge."

I shove my boots haphazardly beneath my bench, almost yank the kitchen door off its hinges in my haste to get through it, and charge up the hall like my ass is on fire.

Bursting into our room, Hope is nowhere to be seen. I crane my head back to look upstairs, but there's no sign of her there either. A gentle breeze disturbs the curtain over the French door and I realise it's ajar. Hope must be in the backyard. Sure enough, she's at the line, feeling each item of laundry to check it's dry, "Hey."

She looks around and beams at me.

"Leave that...come in here for a second. There's something..." I'm practically dancing from foot to foot like a toddler needing to pee. Puzzled, Hope abandons her task and wanders over. As she enters the room, I grip her hand and tug her insistently across the house, up the stairs and straight into the bathroom, shutting and locking the door behind us. She's staring at me as if I've lost my mind, and I guess in a way I have. I cast about the room before making my decision, lifting and plonking her onto the tiled box concealing the toilet cistern. Wide-eyed, mouth open, she gapes at me. I don't pause to question whether this is a good idea, or acceptable behaviour between a husband and wife. I just know it's going to happen here and it has to happen now.

I unfasten the belt of her jeans and fumble with the button and zipper. Unblinking eyes on mine, she pushes down on the shelf with her hands, lifting her body so I can slide off her jeans and panties. I straddle the toilet, unbuckle my belt, push down my own jeans and underwear as far as they'll go. I'm shuddering all over with desire for her. Neither of us has uttered a word. She's still just staring at me.

"Do I look like a madman?"

"Yeah. Your eyes are popping out of your head!"

Voice hoarse, I whisper, "This is happening now, Hope. I can't wait any longer."

Tiptoes on the toilet seat, eyes glittering like jewels, she slowly spreads her legs, wordlessly granting me access to her body. She might as well have roped me, as I lurch across the eighteen inches of space between us, clasp her to me with my left hand in the small of her back, and push the fingers of my right hand inside her. She inhales sharply, and exhales a little moan. Her glorious eyes never leave my face.

It's wet, warm and velvety-soft inside her, and my cock jerks sharply, as if reminding me his turn is well overdue. I push my face into her hair and my penis inside her body. That little noise again. Not a breath, not a sigh, but somewhere in between. Probably the most erotic sound I've ever heard.

The urge to drive hard is all-consuming. It's a physical effort to hold myself back, to move slowly, to let her body become used to my sharp invasion. Each intensifying thrust of mine is met and matched by a corresponding tilting of her pelvis, keeping me deep inside her. Her little hands grip the edge of the shelf, toes of one foot pressing hard onto the toilet seat, the other leg curled around my thigh. We don't talk to one another. There's only our panting breaths and the rhythmic chiming of my belt buckle against the toilet's porcelain side. I can feel the compulsion to ejaculate building irresistibly. The assuredness of my strokes stutters as I fight to hold it back. Hope's arms wrap tight around my neck and she touches her soft cheek to my abrasive one. I slide my hands underneath her buttocks, lifting and holding her to me as she winds her legs around my hips and leans back against the wall. I gasp aloud, shaking my head, eyes closed, head down, body faltering, "No…no…no, come on…"

I'm aware of Hope's moist lips against my ear and her fingers in my hair.

"No…no…too soon…" My body is shuddering again, desperate not to thrust into her, powerless to resist.

Hope exhales a laugh against my cheek, teasing, "Just do it…come on… Ride me, cowboy."

What the hell am I supposed to do about that? Surrender is inevitable. Complete rigidity stands my body to quivering attention for an instant before the heavenly release surges like a tidal wave breaching a dam, carrying me helplessly onward, receding as fast as it arrived to leave me beached, breathless, and so weak my legs buckle beneath me and a giggling Hope has to hold me up. I slump forward onto her, heart thudding, fumbling hands gripping the tiled shelf to support me so she doesn't have to, "Oh, Jesus!" Gasping and grunting against her, limbs juddering, I rest my forehead on hers and fight to recover my breath and balance.

Hope mocks gently, "Are you having a heart attack?"

"Maybe…" I pant, "What a way to go!"

I wrap my arms around her and savour the sensation of resting inside her body, "I'm sorry. I'm not usually that shit, I swear."

She chuckles throatily and the light catches the moisture on her lips, making them glisten like sun on the river. I realise I haven't kissed her yet, not on the mouth, and stroke a finger under her chin, uptilting her face to mine. My lips are millimetres from hers when I hear Hedge's shout, "Boss, you in here? Phone for you! Sir? Are you in the bathroom? They say it's urgent."

His footfalls thud on the stairs. Hope looks horrified, "Is he coming up here to *check*?"

Reluctantly, I ease myself from her, hating the cold on my skin as our bodies part. I yank up my underwear and jeans, frantically tucking in my shirt and buckling my belt.

"Boss? Phone! They say it's real important!"

"It's tough being in demand. See you later."

"Okay."

"Thank you."

"What do you Americans say? 'You're welcome'…"

Her dancing eyes hold mine. I'm tempted to open the door, tell Hedge to stick his urgent 'phone call up his ass, and get right back to it. I whisper, "I could do this all afternoon…"

Hope snorts, "No you couldn't!"

I clutch my chest and stagger backwards, pretending to be mortally wounded by her accuracy as she rocks with silent mirth. I mouth, "Later," unlock the door and let myself out of the bathroom, "Jesus, Hedge, can't I even pee in peace?"

He's already at the top of the stairs. "Sorry, Boss," he points towards the kitchen and the farmhouse 'phone, "There's a call for you. They're holding."

"Okay, Hedge. Thank you. Go on, then." I allow him to precede me down, and blow a secret kiss to my delicious wife as she peeks around the edge of the bathroom door to check the coast is clear.

HOPE

Life settles to a pattern, and not an unpleasant one. I'm gently awoken every morning by my husband with a tray of whatever's for breakfast and my special pot of English tea. He opens the curtains to reveal the majesty of our ever-changing view, plonks the tray on the mattress, and settles down beside me to sip his coffee and chat about the day in prospect. He's so busy I think he's all but forgotten about the cameras, as he never mentions them. I must admit, as I relax into the gentle rhythm of life here, and into the deepening intimacy of our unusual union, I've begun to care a little less about their watching ways, but I'm rarely able to dismiss their presence entirely. I'm sure I could if I had more to *do*...

There it is, then, my only gripe about Ridge River. I'm accepted, adored, and bored to tears. Apart from mealtimes, I barely see Everett. I can go out and find him, and he's always delighted when I do, but it's not a solution. By virtue of being married to the boss, I occupy an elevated position I don't deserve. It prevents me doing anything useful apart from my rostered stint of chores. For the boys, my constant offers of assistance present the quandary of having to dissuade me as politely as possible. They love Everett, but a strict hierarchy is enforced here, and I can see how important that is to the smooth running of the place. I don't want to be the one responsible for inciting rebellion by blurring the boundaries. I respect the way life works here, and I don't want to change it.

We aren't allowed to know about the other couples in this experiment, and only receive the smallest of snapshots of how the show is being received, because the producers rightly conclude knowledge of this kind would alter our behaviour, but we've gleaned enough from Ralton to understand we're the lucky ones. One marriage is reportedly an interminable round of recrimination; the other, polite, distant and dull. In comparison, what we have exceeds every expectation, but I'm nevertheless concerned that the pattern of my first marriage is being repeated here: a driven, busy, successful man, and a frustrated, purposeless, resentful woman. I can't let that happen again, but I don't want to turn into the eternal whinger, whining endlessly about being bored and implying Everett should fix it. I'm Mrs Hope McCann, the gutsy cowgirl with the sassy reflection! It's surely within my own power to alter the trajectory of my life?

Resolving that the best way to gain perspective on a situation is to document it as an observer, I begin a private diary. Not only does it instantly deliver structure to my day, but it rapidly becomes addictive. I start with a few jottings in an old exercise book Melanie digs out for me, but this is soon insufficient for my outpourings. Getting down all the entertaining, interesting and downright quirky things that happen here keeps me scribbling from breakfast 'til lunch. I then get and out about, either on Mariah or on foot, ensuring I'm not missing anything, which more than adequately fills an afternoon. I take endless pictures on my 'phone, and Everett lets me use his laptop to type everything up. I ask Nathan the teenage hacker how best to combine words and pictures into an electronic diary for my own amusement, and he shows me how to start a Blog. I'm nervous of the fact it's on the internet, so anyone could see it, but am comforted by the knowledge that no one else knows it's there. Within a few short weeks, I'm hooked, happily-absorbed in the creation, design, editing and uploading of my posts and pictures, each a little reportage article with a chosen theme, the underlying thread of ranch life running through every piece like the eternal fast-flowing river. It makes me wonder what life would have been like if I'd actually pursued a journalism career, but the fact that this is secret, has no deadline, no audience and no editor makes for an unrealistic comparison. Who cares? Right now, I'm the healthiest, happiest and most free I've been since I packed my suitcase for the first term of University, aged eighteen. I made up my mind I'd fix my own problem, and I have! My writing doesn't earn me any money, and I'm still very conscious of being financially-beholden to yet another husband, but I've finally found something I can actually *do*.

****

"Where's it hurting?"

Everett scowls and indicates all the areas of discomfort: shoulder blade, shoulder joint, down his left-hand side, left arm, across his collarbone, down the side of his neck

"Everywhere, then?"

"Pretty much."

"Can't they do anything for you?"

He shakes his head, "I'm lucky to have any use of my left arm at all. The pain is a reminder that I should have gotten an office job."

I ruffle his hair affectionately, "Can't imagine you in an office."

"Me neither."

"Sit forward a bit so I can reach down your back. Do I rub this stuff between my hands and then slap it on, or do I put it straight on you?"

"I don't think it matters, as long as you rub it right in."

"Okay," I squidge a blob of the ointment between my palms and rub them together, "Oh, you can feel the heat off it!"

"It's clever stuff. Mo's Mom boils it up at home."

"You should find out what she puts in it."

"I might not wanna know…"

I giggle as I smooth my palms across Everett's suntanned skin, stroking rhythmically in a gentle motion alternately up his oblique to his shoulder and down his arm, or over the lines of raised scar-tissue across his shoulder blade to his collarbone and up the side of his neck. My greased hands glide, every slight movement as he fidgets with the discomfort of pressure on his sore body causing a firm muscle to tighten pleasurably beneath my fingers. The sensation of the movement, the warmth, the gentle back and forth as I smooth up and stretch down has a hypnotic effect upon me. My eyes glaze, my breathing slows, and I'm only aware of the heat of the connection between my sliding hands and his taut body.

Everett leans back suddenly, surprising me. I yelp, "Mind the chair! You'll get ointment on it!"

His eyes are half-closed. There's a lazy smile playing around his lips, "That feels so nice…"

"Is it getting rid of the ache?"

"Oh yeah… Trouble is, it's causing an ache somewhere else instead…"

I snigger and push him upright with my hands on his shoulders, "Sit forward, you'll wreck the chair!"

I begin the gentle motion again, and Everett sighs deeply.

"What should I rub on the new ache?"

Everett chuckles, "Yourself, preferably."

Easing my hands up the left-hand side of his thick neck, I ask, "How's that feel now? Want me to stop?"

"No, are you *crazy*?"

Gratified, I dip a finger into the jar, smear another bed of ointment onto my palms, continue. After a while, the slow rocking motion as I massage makes my trapped feet tingle, pins and needles pricking them uncomfortably. I wriggle them from underneath me, dangling my legs down next to Everett's shoulders, numb limbs throbbing as the blood flow returns. Everett cups my right foot in his huge palm, "Your feet are cold."

"It's 'cos my legs are so long. My heart just can't pump the blood that far."

"You keep telling yourself that."

A moment of contented silence elapses before he drawls sleepily, "You know, this is the thing I love the most."

"What, constant physical pain?"

"Being taken *care* of. All my life, it's been me doing the looking after. There's never been anyone to care for me...until you."

I pat his shoulder, "And you take care of me in return, and that's what marriage means."

"I love it. I love *all* of it."

"So do I."

Everett squeezes my foot, drawing a finger down the length of the sole, making my toes curl and twitch as it tickles. He turns his head to observe the camera in the corner of the room, its black lens trained on us. I pull his earlobe gently, "What are you thinking?"

"I'm thinking would we really be breaking the rules if something were to 'accidentally' drop over the lens?"

"We're not supposed to cover them!"

"I know...but if I get hold of you like I want to, you're gonna go, 'No, Everett, the cameras!'"

I pout at his impression, "Not necessarily..."

"Bullshit."

"No, it's not!"

"Okay..." calling my bluff, he turns, kneels up before my chair, leans forward to kiss me. My eyes flit from his face to the camera before I can prevent them and he starts to laugh, running his big, warm hands the length of my thighs from knees to hips, reaching up, pushing my hair aside and kissing my neck instead. His exhaled laughter tickles my skin. Now, I'm giggling too, but hesitant nonetheless, "How can you do this with that *thing* watching?"

His huge hands cup my buttocks, squeeze, slide me closer, "Baby, the way I feel about you, I could do it on the pitch at the Superbowl."

His questing fingers tug at the belt of my dressing gown, loosening the knot, preparing to part the fabric. I'm naked beneath it. Before he can uncover me, I slap my ointment-coated palms against his beautiful bare chest, "Okay, you win! I admit it. I still can't do it right in front of the camera."

Triumphantly, "Told ya! We shoulda had twenty bucks on it!"

I glare at him, tightly retying the loosened belt.

He sniggers, indicates his erection, "What now?"

Poker-faced, "Scrabble?"

Everett grabs for the front of my dressing gown as if he's going to whip it open, and I squeak and frantically clutch at the two sides of the robe, causing him to rock back on his heels with a rich roar of laughter.

"Seriously, is that it? 'C'mere Big Boy…no, actually, I've changed my mind, let's rearrange your sock drawer instead'?"

"Oh, that's not a bad idea. You've got loads with big holes in that you *insist* on wearing…"

"That ain't even funny!"

I smirk at his tetchy expression as he demands, "Well?"

It's titillating to be in charge of this. I smile, ease upright, whisper in his ear, "Turn the chair round."

"What?"

"Point the back of the chair at the camera."

"For real? And then we're game on?"

"Yes."

"It'll still be in front of the camera, Hope."

"But it's a big chair with a high back."

"You promise?"

"Cross my heart."

Everett does an exaggerated fist-pump, and pulls the large chair round on the tiled floor. It scrapes slightly. I wince, "I could get up…?"

"No, you stay right there. You're not escaping. You *promised* me."

Repositioned, he asks, "Happy?"

I peek around the high, winged side. The camera lens still stares…hopefully only at the boring leather back of the massive armchair.

"Happy…"

"Come here, then."

One yank dispenses with the belt of my dressing gown, and impatient hands throw aside the overlaps of material, reaching for me. The silky robe slithers away and drops back onto the seat as Everett lifts my naked body to his. I slide my hands around his shoulders and down his back, "You're all greasy."

He grins, "So will you be in a minute."

We're both laughing even as we kiss. I wrap my legs around him, using their weight to pull his body down onto mine, "My gorgeous husband."

Everett sighs contentedly, holds me tight, whispers, "My beautiful wife."

"Can life get any better than this?"

He kisses me gently, "I doubt it."

Members of the 'FIRST SIGHT' Production Team:
RACHEL DELANEY – Executive Producer
DIANA MAURICE – Programme Consultant

Rachel: It rapidly became the cutest thing on television. Hard-bitten old critics were gushing over it in reviews. Vasquez and I were surreptitiously clearing a space on the shelf in the office for our Emmy.

Diana: Regardless of what happened later on, I think we can all take a little credit for bringing together two people who did genuinely fall in love with one another. In that respect, I believe the show was an unqualified success.

Rachel: Absolutely! I mean, do you remember the stuff with the chair?

Diana: Oh, so *sweet!*

Rachel: Everett had these two huge wing-back chairs in front of the fire, but they only ever really used one.

Diana: They used to curl up in it together and just gaze at one another, as if they truly couldn't believe what was happening to them.

Rachel: It was superb tv because it was so wonderful to edit. We'd cut between the three couples: Monica and Bill having this very stilted, paint-dryingly dull conversation over dinner; Regis and Sylvie screaming and throwing things at each other, and Everett and Hope curled up in their chair together, lost in one another, with just the crackling of the fire... I mean, it was super-cute.

Diana: Reportedly, sales of that style of armchair soared over that Christmas, didn't they?

Rachel: Yeah, we should've had merchandising rights on those! What about the t-shirts?

Diana: I still *have* one!

Rachel: So do *I*! Some enterprising soul – again, to my lasting regret, nothing to do with the show – made up t-shirts printed with a big armchair, a cushion on it in the shape of a heart, and the legend: 'I love you like Everett loves Hope'.

Diana: And *everyone* knew what it meant!

Rachel: I should've considered merch, but I never realised how much of a phenomenon they'd become. Before long, two thirds of each transmission was devoted to the McCann's, with the other two couples crammed into the remaining third, if we actually had time to feature them at all. It was essentially the Everett and Hope show. Fledgling social media was alight with it. Shortly after, these Blog links started to persistently appear on my twitter feed. I was dimly aware that Hope was doing some kind of internet diary, but there was so much else happening, I hadn't paid much attention to it. Suddenly, I realised half my social feed was full of people name-checking and sharing this adorable Blog...and it was Hope's! There she was, setting the world alight on the page as well as on the screen, and she was capturing thousands more subscribers every week. My 'phone starting ringing, and the offers began to flood in. It presented me with the kind of incredible problem you normally only dream of, that of being *too* successful. Everyone wanted a slice of Hope, and they could only get to her through me. The issue I had was, if I told her what was happening, it would straightaway undermine the integrity of the show…and I couldn't do that. The show was my baby. It was *my* original idea, and it had been two years of my life in the planning. But I was also starting to understand that the whole thing was spiralling out of my control. I had a decision to make that would affect a lot of lives, and not necessarily for the better.

HOPE

I'm feeling penned-in by the bad weather. The Christmas season here is magical, but the snow comes in hard by November, bringing high winds and blizzards that imprison us inside. I've got so used to being out and about in endless pursuit of inspiration that being stuck indoors drives me potty with frustration as one day turns to two, three, four, and the drifting snow climbs higher up the windowpanes. I venture out bundled like a polar explorer, but the extremity of the cold drives me back inside.

Before New Year, the mercury plunges and the waterfall freezes, its cascade hardening to a creaking, cracking mass. It feels as if I've gone deaf, and I realise how accustomed I've become to the constant rumble of the water. A few days later, the weather breaks, allowing some respite from the punishing minus-twenties of wind chill. Fog-bound since breakfast, lunchtime delivers a sudden shaft of milky sunlight, stretching across the kitchen wall and making everyone twitchy. Bundled against the sub-zero cold, we all spill out onto the powdery paths, blowing away our individual cobwebs in the crisp air.

I skid and stumble down the rocky path to the river. On my arrival in late summer, the riverbank had been a riot of wildflowers and dry grasses rippling in the warm breezes funnelled up the valley from the wide prairie, now entombed beneath three feet of pristine snow. The opposite bank is criss-crossed with animal tracks. I step from the path and take childish pleasure in the creation of my own pattern of equidistant footprints all the way to the water's edge. The river, so clear and inviting on a hot day, looks dark and sinister now. I squat in the inch of trickling water to investigate what it is between the stones that's catching the slanting rays of sunshine. Fascinated, I slip off a glove and stroke a finger across the minute ice-bridges nature has constructed between each stone. Beneath these tiny feats of engineering, the river tinkles musically around the pebbles, flowing too determinedly to freeze.

Unsure how long I've crouched here, I become aware how cold my feet are, and that the hand I'm trailing dreamily along the pleasantly tactile little flyovers of ice is throbbing from exposure. I ease upright, wincing, and limp in erratic circles to stimulate my reluctant circulation, flattening the snow around me and ruining its perfection.

I trudge purposefully along the riverbank in the direction of the waterfall. Here, the snow is deeper. Gusts of wind have driven it into high drifts against the ridge. From the lowest bending branches of the pines, exploratory stalactites of ice indent these mounds of snow with perfect circles, like a fingertip into a cone of flour.

The powdery snow overtops my boots and coats my trousers. The fabric sticks to my complaining skin, making an unpleasant, cold ring around my knees. Foolish to get wet, I now need to hurry home whether I'm ready to or not. I make for the next trail. The drifts are at their worst here, some thigh deep. It's a relief to grasp a protruding branch and pull myself onto the rocky path, shaking the thickest of the crystals from my clothes before they make me wetter and colder than I already am.

The steep uphill trudge warms me once more, and I arrive on the plateau sweaty and puffing, head itchy beneath my woolly hat. As I wander into the clearing, I'm surprised to see the firepit has been recently used. Embers still smoulder, trails of smoke meandering upwards. One of the boys must have lit it. They bring guests here on rides when the weather isn't quite so harsh, sitting them around the campfire to drink hot chocolate and photograph the view. A rough-and-ready woodpile is stacked behind one of the trees. I scoop an armful of kindling and use a robust-looking stick as a poker, clumping the brightest embers together and steepling a few twigs above them, blowing optimistically on the ashes until they smoke promisingly. A spark catches at the dead bark curling from one piece of wood. The orange flame spirals tantalisingly around the curl, blackening it, but it doesn't catch. Disappointed, I lean over again, puffing with rhythmic force, rewarded for my effort by a licking tongue of flame. To my satisfaction, it tickles up the closest piece of wood and begins its determined consumption of the fuel. As this stick catches, the ones next to it follow. Soon, my teepee of twigs collapses into a merry little blaze in the centre of the ring of stones. Pleased, I hurry back to the woodpile and fetch more.

Perched on a log, occasionally feeding my hungry little fire with morsels of wood, I contemplate the vista before me. It reminds me of Christmas cakes my mother used to bake. In the leaching daylight, the black river in the snowy landscape is a ribbon of liquorice across fondant icing, the lines of snow-covered pines so many jellies standing upright in clusters, calling to be picked off with tiny fingers and eaten surreptitiously. The centrepiece of my youth would have been a fondant Santa, whose consumption was only permitted once the cake was cut. Here, it's the stunning backdrop of the craggy, snow-covered mountains, their faces turned as pink by tonight's sunset as they'd been on the day I first arrived here. Not much call for fondant mountains on the London Christmas cakes of the 1980s, but maybe they're on every homemade creation in Wyoming? Like the waterfall, they form a ubiquitous backdrop to my life here. That's quite some majesty to already take for granted. The view out of my bedsit window had been the rear brick wall and fire escape of the neighbouring building. They were so close together you had to kneel on the floor and squish your face against the pane just to catch a glimpse of sky. Here, it's endless, stretching off across the prairie to the distant horizon, tempting you to mosey on down and sneak a peek at whatever's over the next hill. There's always another trail to follow, another hill to climb, another stream to ford, another prairie to cross.

A huge shiver convulses my body. I need to make my way home before it's completely dark, but I'm loathe to leave the warmth of my comforting little fire. I pile on the remaining wood at my feet. When the flames devour it all, I'll go back.

Bending forward, the toe of my boot topples a little stone cairn. Absently, I begin to restack it. Absorbed in my task, I'm unaware of my wandering thoughts until they settle upon one image, that of Justin's adorable red-haired son, so intently piling potatoes on the supermarket floor. Hot tears rush into my eyes and my gloved fingers falter, dropping the stone I'm holding, tumbling the teetering pyramid again.

"Oh!"

The exclamation sounds too much like a sob in the silent clearing. I almost jump out of my skin as my husband's big arms envelop me, and his warm face presses my frozen skin to kiss my cheek, "Hey, are you *crying?*"

"What?"

"You had no idea I was here, did you?"

"No," I sniff and fidget, distressed and embarrassed in equal measure.

"It's freezing. What you doing here in the dark?"

"I had to get outside. I was sick of being indoors…"

"You gonna tell me what the matter is?"

I rest my head against his shoulder. He strokes my cheek with his gloved hand.

"It's silly, Everett."

"Tell me anyway."

"Someone's built a little sculpture, look."

"And that made you cry? Never knew you were an art critic."

He's so good at this, standing me up when I stumble.

"Justin's baby. I saw him once, in the supermarket. They didn't see me. I watched the baby making little piles of potatoes on the floor while no one was looking. He had bright red hair. He could have been *mine*! It shook me up so badly I went home and drank most of a bottle of neat vodka and made myself puke. He was living, breathing, gorgeous proof that everyone else's life was marching successfully on except mine. It was the final straw. I filled in that application form faster than you can say 'mid-life crisis'."

"Are you telling me you regret it now? You're only with me because of trauma and vodka?"

"The memory hurt, Everett, that's all. It crept up on me when I was least expecting it."

"I'm sorry... It's the one thing I can't give you, no matter how hard I try."

"It's not your fault, is it? It's mine."

He hugs me closer, "It's no one's *fault*, Hope. It's just bad luck. You can't rail against shit when there's no fixing it. What's the point in that?"

"I know. I didn't *deliberately* think about it at all. Come on. We need to get back. I want to get changed for Jesse and Mel's latest gutfest...even though I'm not actually not sure I can force down yet another massive dinner."

"I eat way too much every Christmas. That's what you're *meant* to do, isn't it?"

I struggle to my feet, "Well, I *know* I've put on weight. My trousers are getting *really* tight."

EVERETT

"You okay?"

"Mmmm…?"

"Tired?"

"Little bit…why?"

"You look pale. You've got dark rings under your eyes…"

"Is this your subtle way of telling me I look a fright or something?"

"I just think you look tired, that's all. Still beautiful…but tired…"

Luckily, Hope sniggers at this. It could so easily have escalated into a fight, her taking offence I didn't mean at a criticism I wasn't making. She's been touchy recently, unreasonable, snappy, and then there's the eating thing. She put some weight on over Christmas, seemed to get self-conscious about it, and now I'm worried she's starving herself to lose it again. She's certainly been tired and listless since the year turned. That's why I've brought her to the steakhouse, to get away from home, from the cameras she still hates, and convince her to eat a good meal for the first time in a month.

"I think I might have a burger, fries, coleslaw… What do you want, honey? Want a steak?"

Hope swallows suddenly, shakes her head silently, sips slowly at her water.

"Baby, you gotta eat. Have something light. Have a tuna salad or something…"

She winces, as if discussion of the menu is distasteful, "I've no appetite to be honest, Ev."

No wife of mine is developing some kind of goddam eating disorder, "Hope, I don't know what's gotten into you since New Year, but you need to eat. Just pick something small. How about a sandwich? A tomato salad?"

I'm dimly aware of a figure appearing at the end of our booth, and naturally assume it's the waitress. I glance up, about to ask for another minute, but it isn't the waitress standing there. It's a middle-aged woman in a purple blouse, who's clutching a beer mat in both her hands and jigging around as if she's desperate to talk but too nervous to do so. I've seen the behaviour before, although admittedly not for a while. It's the attitude of someone who wants an autograph but isn't sure how to ask.

"May we help you, Ma'am?"

"It *is* you! I just had to check. From over there we thought it was you. We just weren't sure because you had your back to us...but we figured it must be!"

I glance behind and observe a table of five other women, shining, expectant faces turned towards us. I flash my most charismatic smile in their direction, and am just about to ask if anyone has a pen when I realise none of them are showing the remotest interest in me. This table of delighted, gushing, starstruck ladies don't give a damn about Everett McCann the faded champ. It's Hope's autograph they want.

Hope's smile is bemused, putting down her water glass and reaching for her handbag, "Do you really want me to sign that mat? I've got a notebook in here. I could sign a page of that instead?"

She slides further into the booth, pats the bench next to her, "Sit down for a second. It's in here somewhere..." rooting up to her elbow in the capacious bag. The woman sits with alacrity, mouthing 'Oh My God!' towards her friends, who have stopped beaming and are now gawping open-mouthed, as if their buddy's just been invited to sit on the Queen of England's knee.

"Ah, here we go!" Triumphant, Hope yanks the notebook she's never without from the murky depths of her bag, opening it to the centrefold and loosening the staples so she can ease out a couple of pages without them ripping, "Whom shall I make it out to?" craning to address the watching table, "Do you all want one? I'm not accustomed to this. What do I put?"

Before I have time to decide whether it's entertaining or inconvenient, my wife vanishes in a huddle of bent female heads, all gathered around requesting personalised messages, asking questions and generally worshipping at the altar of Hope McCann. I can't blame them, I've been prostrated there for months, and am similarly in no hurry to leave.

At least when the waitress does appear, I'm able to order our food without Hope complaining about what I choose. I do get a little irritated when the meal arrives and they're all still crowded around gassing. I don't want to eat with them there, but my stomach growls with anticipation, no one is taking a blind bit of notice of me, so in the end I just start.

I've nearly finished by the time they quit gossiping and leave us in peace. One positive outcome is their flattering attention has perked Hope up, lifting her out of her lethargy. She willingly takes bites of the sandwich she said she didn't want, and pierces slices of mozzarella and tomato on her fork...but I notice when she claims to have finished, only half of the sandwich is gone. She's cheerful, and livelier than she's seemed in a while, so I don't make it a big deal, "Dessert?"

She wrinkles her nose, "I've gone off sweet stuff. Too much at Christmas, probably."

"Shall I get the check? What do you wanna do, go for a drink somewhere...?"

Hope yawns wide behind her hand, blinking at me like she does at five in the morning when I wake her accidentally, "Let's just go home and snuggle in bed."

"Sure thing."

I look up, but fail to catch the eye of the waitress. What *is* it tonight with women ignoring me? Maybe you hit fifty and the charm you've relied upon since adolescence evaporates like a puddle in the midday sun? I grin at Hope, "I'm invisible tonight."

She winks at me, "You shouldn't be so average."

My fragile self-confidence teeters…but she's kidding, right?

"So, what were you and the Fan Club talking about so animatedly?"

"You were there!"

"I'm a guy! I was eating! You know we can't do more than one thing at a time. Anyway, you were all squawking over one another and I couldn't make out a word. You know you talk a different language, don't you?"

Hope puts on an exaggerated accent, and enunciates, "What, the Queen's English?"

I laugh, "Woman."

"What?"

"Woman. It's a foreign tongue men don't fully understand."

Hope rolls her eyes, "They all watch the show!"

"I got *that* part."

"I said I wasn't allowed to know much about it, but they said nearly everyone they *know* watches it!"

"You're kidding? I definitely missed that bit!"

"Yeah…and I told them not to reveal anything, but they sort of hinted that we were best!" Hope beams so gleefully I can't help but smile back, "Of *course* we're best!"

"They also said their absolute favourite bit is when you walk around the house with no shirt on, so I've promised to hide half your wardrobe to ensure it happens more frequently."

Blushing, laughing, I confess, "It's kinda weird, huh? All those ladies have seen me in my underwear…"

"Yes, and it seems to make them *very* happy."

She reaches across the table and slips her slim fingers between mine, "It makes *me* very happy too."

"Well, I only care about what you think…"

Hope yawns again, "Can we go home?"

"Sure." This time, I successfully attract the attention of the waitress with my accustomed ease, and mime wanting the check. The Hope Appreciation Society turn to wave as we leave, saluting as one with their raised dessert spoons.

Hope slides her arm around my waist and presses herself tight against my side, shivering as we leave the warmth of the restaurant and step out onto the snowy sidewalk, "Just imagine…six horny housewives, one Everett, and a bucket of ice-cream sundae. Would you know what to do with yourself?"

"Stop it, or I'll be too shy to come into town ever again!"

Hope laughs delightedly, enjoying teasing me. I revel in it. She hasn't been like this much over the last few weeks.

"You know what else they said that was really nice?"

"What's that?"

We reach the truck and I open Hope's door for her. As I get in, start the truck, pull away, the tyres skid briefly on the piled ice at the side of the road. The vehicle judders, grips with a roar of the big engine, then we're free of the mini snowdrift and out onto the ploughed main drag. Hope fiddles with the blowers and switches on the heated seat, teeth chattering, "When did you say the snow melts?"

"April…"

Hope tuts glumly and settles into thoughtful silence, bundled in her coat.

Eventually, I get sick of waiting, "You can't stop halfway through a sentence!"

"I forgot what I was talking about!"

"The nicest thing your Fan Club said…?"

"Oh yeah! That they all subscribe to my Blog, and they know other people who do too. Sandy – the one in the purple top – said a lady in her office has saved up and booked to come to the hotel for a week in the spring for her twenty-fifth wedding anniversary! We need to remember to tell Mel."

"Because of the show?"

Hope presses her lips together momentarily, before bashfully admitting, "Because of my Blog, Sandy said."

"Your internet thing?"

"Yeah."

"I didn't know you had people following it. I just thought you did it for your own amusement."

"I did…but some people cottoned on to it, and now I've got subscribers."

"That's cool. How many do you have?"

Her tone is so casual it takes a moment to sink in when she breezes, "Was just over two hundred thousand when I went on there yesterday…two hundred and two thousand, or something like that."

"…Two hundred *thousand*?"

I turn to gape at her and the truck swerves across the mercifully-empty street.

Hope squeaks, "Everett!"

"Sorry." I straighten us up, but can't help staring at her, head swivelling repeatedly from my constantly surprising wife to the snowy road in front of us, darkening as we leave town.

"What are you staring at?"

I jerk my head, "Get over here!"

Grinning quizzically, Hope slides across the bench seat and snuggles against me, putting her arms around my body.

"You have two hundred thousand people subscribing to what you write about our ranch?"

"Yes. At first, I just liked the idea that people were interested – and I get lovely feedback – but then Mel was talking about bookings being down because apparently the show is putting off all those A-list twats who 'don't want to be on camera', despite non-stop attention being the backbone of their needy little lives. Anyway, I felt bad, because it's sort of our fault isn't it?"

"No! I *refuse* to take the blame, even though Melanie was desperately trying to pin it on me. I spoke to both of them about this thing before I ever signed the contract. They thought I was nuts, but they also believed it would be great publicity."

"I thought, if my Blog had grown so well organically, without any promotion at all, how much better could it do if I *pushed* it a bit?"

"And people like Sandy's friend are *already* booking to spend their special anniversaries with us..."

"Nice, isn't it? Makes me feel warm inside that Ridge River is someone's special treat they'll remember forever, instead of just another bougie tick-box destination for people who don't appreciate it because they're *accustomed* to comfort, and luxury, and getting their arses kissed..."

"I'm continually concerned I'm underestimating you at every turn. Those women tonight were so excited just to stand next to you, because you can enchant two hundred thousand fans with words on a screen! That's some power you've got. I'm pretty scared of all that potential."

"Scared?"

"Yeah! You're just at the start of this! The way you're talking, minimal effort on your part and a whole stack of people are bewitched. What could you achieve if you *really* tried? Jesus, Hope, world domination's on the cards here! Is it any wonder it's striking terror into me?"

"I don't understand..."

"How can I ever compete with that?"

"What?"

"You're going places, Hope, can you not see that? Places I don't have the intellect to imagine! How long before you decide this sleepy backwater and your hick of a husband just ain't quite hitting the spot any more?"

Hope sits up abruptly, pulling away from me, "Stop the car!"

I pull over to the side of the empty road. She grips hold of my head and yanks me roughly round to face her, panting with emotion, "Never, *never* say that! You *are* enough! You have been since the start! You always *will* be, Everett! Where is this coming from?" Her wide, frightened eyes shine in the muted dashboard light, fearfully raking my face.

"You've been so preoccupied since Christmas. Kinda low. I was worried it was something *I'd* done...and then tonight happened and I'm starting to realise it was actually something I could *never* do. All the things you sacrificed to your first marriage are coming to you now, and you've already told me you won't let another husband stand in your way. That was fine by me all the while there was nothing to stand in the way of...but now there is, right? Now there's Sandy and all her buddies, and two hundred thousand other people too! How can I possibly compete with that?"

****

Lunch over, it's only Hope and I left in the kitchen. It's her day on cooking duty, and she's washing the dishes while I stand before the whiteboard with my marker pen, trying to plan out work for the next few days. The ring of high heels on the tack room tiles announces Melanie, who bursts breathlessly into the kitchen.

Hope looks round from the sink, "Hello, you!"

With pretend gruffness, I point aggressively, "No outdoor shoes in the house!"

Melanie shakes her head irritably, as if she really doesn't have time for my nonsense, snapping, "These are Jimmy Choo. They're hardly covered in horse shit!"

"Jimmy who? Did you walk across the yard?"

"Yes...?"

"Then they're covered in horse shit."

Melanie waves an elegant hand dismissively, "Will you shut up?"

"What do you want, anyway?"

"Sorry, Mr Indispensable, but I need Hope, not you."

"What?" Hope, suds up her forearms, is trying to look round at Mel whilst still washing, and fumbles a slippery plate. It smacks back into the sink and slops a wave of soapy water up the front of her blouse, "Oh, bloody hell!"

She grabs for the tea-towel and pats ineffectually, too soaked for it to make any difference, "What's up, Mel?"

Melanie perches on the corner of the table, "I don't have time for long explanations. You need to smarten yourself up a bit and come back down to the lodge with me. I have some people who are *desperate* to meet you!"

"Who?"

"Fans! Come on, Hope. Forget the damn dishes! Everett can do 'em."

"Oh, *can* he?"

Melanie delivers the unimpressed look she reserves for me alone, "Yes. He can."

Hope is looking from me to Mel and back again like a spectator at a tennis match. Melanie rounds upon her, "Come on, Hope! Don't just stand there catching flies, go get changed! And brush your hair!"

Melanie bundles the baffled Hope down the hall and turns back into the kitchen, eyes shining, "She's a celebrity! This couple today have just checked in and wouldn't stop going on about her! They were asking if she was here, and if they'd get to catch a glimpse of her while they were staying…so I casually asked if they'd like to meet her…? You'd have thought I'd just told 'em next week's lottery numbers! They're only here because of her…and they're the *fifth* couple this month to name-check her Blog on their booking! I looked at the website, and three-quarters of our enquiries now come through her site, not ours!"

Usually I'm pretty confident about the truth, depth and origin of my feelings, so the ambivalence I'm experiencing is a new phenomenon. On the one hand, I'm bursting with pride. On the other, the same terror that gripped me in the truck on the way home from the steakhouse stampedes through my body like a herd across a plain. Here comes the outside world, threatening the tranquil peace of our union with its glittering temptations. I quash the fear with effort, trying to focus solely on the pride, "Do you know, she has two hundred *thousand* people subscribing to her Blog?"

"I think it's more than that now…and have you read it?"

"Of course I've read it! I totally support everything she does!" I protest a little too vehemently.

"Isn't it *wonderful*, Everett? It just sucks you in. Whoever would guess she was writing about this dump?" Mel's eyes roam the workaday kitchen judgementally, "Everyone's falling over themselves to come!"

Hope reappears in the kitchen in clean jeans, a silk blouse and high heels. Her glossy hair flames in the sunlight. Mel claps her hands together in satisfaction, "Much better! Come on, hurry up!"

She's out into the tack room without bothering to bid me any sort of farewell. Hope glances across the kitchen, wearing the same mystified expression she's had since Mel's arrival. I wink at her, cross my fingers. From outside, Melanie roars, "HOPE! Come *on*!"

My wife shakes her head, shrugs at me, and follows the indefatigable Mrs Cole. I sigh as the sound of excited female voices fades. The empty farmhouse is suddenly very quiet. I can hear the clock ticking and the camera motor whirring as it turns to observe me. In the absence of anyone more fascinating to watch, McCann, I guess you'll do.

Getting the whiteboard finished now is out of the question. I can't think straight enough to make sensible plans. My hands are shaking. It's pathetic, but I'm unnerved by what's happening here. I've never had anything so precious. I simply *cannot* lose her. I think it might kill me if I do. I toss the marker back into the pot on the dresser, roll up my sleeves, and get on with the dishes. At least I'm still good for something.

RACHEL DELANEY
EXECUTIVE PRODUCER 'FIRST SIGHT'

Things reached a climax, a sort of a tipping point, and at the ideal time.

Far from being a tragic end, it was the wonderful beginning of an adventure that turned out to have much greater longevity, and deliver more success and value than any of us could have envisaged when we first set out to make a silly little reality show.

Maybe that's when you know something's truly meant to be, when it all falls into place so perfectly it's like you planned it that way all along...

HOPE

"Rachel, what are *you* doing here? Have we done something we're not supposed to?"

"No, Hope, it's nothing like that. I've brought a crew. I hope you don't mind…?" Rachel gestures behind her to the camera team, who raise hands in silent greeting but don't stop filming.

"What difference does one *more* lens make?"

Rachel exchanges one significant glance with the camera team, "Can we come in, Hope, or not?"

I tut impatiently, hurt she feels she has to ask, "Of course you can come in, don't be daft!"

I help Rachel off with her good-quality overcoat as the crew shuffle into position at one end of the kitchen table, shedding jackets and dumping bags onto the sofa behind them.

The house is empty, all the boys out in the harsh intensity of the biting February gale until dinner time.

"Sit down, Rachel. Can I get you a drink? Something warming? A tea…coffee…?"

I'm talking so Rachel can't. She's got a funny look on her face and it's making me nervous. She plonks down with a dejection quite unlike her usual restless energy, splaying her skinny arms across the kitchen table, hanging her head in an attitude of uncharacteristic defeat. I give her a moment, pretending I haven't noticed, laying out a tray with sufficient cups for everyone in the crew to help themselves. I ease down onto the bench opposite Rachel and edge her mug across the wood towards her until its heat touches her fingertips, rousing her. She smiles gratefully and curls her cold fingers around the hot cup, cradling it. The steam mists her glasses. She asks, "Remind me, where's Everett gone?"

"Down south with Jesse at a machinery show. Back tomorrow."

"Have you missed him?"

"Of course. A lot."

She manages an odd, nervous smile, "You two are so cute, Hope."

"Are we?"

"For sure."

There's such a sad look on her face I can't help but blurt, "What's up, Rach? You seem very distracted. Not your usual punchy self at all."

"Oh, Hope…I don't know how best to say this, so I'm just going to go for it. Sorry in advance if it blows your mind."

"What?"

"It's all over."

"*What?*"

Rachel's chin wobbles slightly. Her cheeks redden. I gawp in unconcealed astonishment.

"Little Sylvie went AWOL three weeks ago with no explanation, and then it came out she'd left Regis and gone back to France. I've not spoken to him, but Diana has. Reportedly, he's delighted to see the back of her! As for Monica and Bill…you remember Tamika from the production crew?"

I shrug. Perhaps I remember her or maybe I've chosen not to, just lumping her in with the gaggle of Everett's giggling New York admirers.

"Turns out Tamika started having a thing with Bill during final selection. It's no wonder a romance never got going between he and Monica, because he was screwing Tamika before the contracts were even *signed*! He came clean to Monica a couple of days ago. It's the most interesting goddam thing he's done on film since this joke started! Needless to say, Tamika quit before she was fired. *That* was the love story, going on in secret under our goddam noses while we were bemoaning the absence of any on-screen spark! She took her wages every month and mouthed platitudes about what it shame it was that Bill and Monica weren't working out…and all the while…!"

Rachel thumps her mug onto the table top, slopping coffee down the sides. I reach for a cloth and mop up as she sinks her head into her hands, groaning, "Oh God, if I *ever* see the three of them again…!"

Alarmed by her anguish, I reach across and squeeze her forearm gently, "Chin up, Rach, it's only telly."

She glares at me coldly, "It's my *career*, Hope, and it was building very nicely, thank you…until this car crash!"

"Sorry…"

"…No, *I'm* sorry. The network big shots had a meeting…and the fact is, they're pulling the plug, Hope."

"What?"

"All contracts null-and-void. No show, no five hundred grand."

"What?"

"Stop saying 'what'!"

"Well, I can't believe it!"

"I'm sorry, Hope, I truly am. It's only been you and Everett holding this thing together from the start, so I feel more for you than any of the others. Only you and Everett have been in this for real and given it your best shot. That's *why* I'm sorry, because you're getting dumped and it's nothing to do with either of you. Vasquez and I were in the meeting. We fought real hard for you. The social media stuff is where it's at, but none of them understand. They're dinosaurs! They don't realise how many people subscribe to your Blog already. They don't see how everyone follows with fascination the ups and downs of life here at Ridge River. I, for one, am totally addicted, but they don't get it! They said the internet stuff was 'too niche' and they weren't prepared to continue financing the expense of the production for the one couple whose 'excuse for a marriage was limping on'."

"Excuse for a marriage?"

A fat tear shoots down Rachel's flat cheek and splats audibly onto the table. She does everything at a gallop, even crying. I reach across and grab her bony hand, squeezing it in mine. She tries to smile, "It was a harsh, frank meeting. I was shaking all over by the time I came out of it. Everyone's been transferred onto other projects. I was supposed just to Skype you…but I've been doing a lot of thinking over the past couple of days…" Rachel purses her lips and trails a manicured fingernail down a grain line in the wooden kitchen table, before prodding a knot hole with a decisive fingertip like she's pressing a launch button.

"I've been withholding something from you, Hope, because I couldn't decide on the best course of action. In my defence, the show is my baby! It was my original idea, and I've been the driving force behind the project from the start. The last thing I wanted was to see it founder, because it meant I'd failed in what I set out to do…but the show *has* failed, despite my very best efforts to keep it going, so there's nothing to stop me doing what I've come here for today."

Rachel reaches to pick up her briefcase. She lifts it onto the bench beside her, unzips it, begins to extract thick sheaves of paperwork bound with legal ribbon and festooned with rustling signature-indicator tags. These are followed by chunky proposal documents with professional-looking binding and logo-plastered covers, issues of glossy magazines with email printouts clipped to the fronts, and numerous other sheets of stapled paperwork. She spreads them haphazardly across the kitchen table until the wooden surface is as buried beneath a thick layer of white as the snow-covered yard outside.

"I've been holding back for the right time, and this is it." She points randomly, "Here, here, here: book deals. This one's a regular *New York Times* column. This one is to write lifestyle travel features for *Condé Nast*. This is features for *Harpers*. Oh, this one's a book deal, too. This is cable tv, chat show slot. This is internet radio, same kind of chat show/magazine programme format..."

She fans a thick pile of papers held together with a bulldog clip, "These are all features on you personally: photo shoots, magazine articles, radio interviews, tv appearances, speaking engagements... I've kept it all simmering on your behalf. The better the Blog performs, the more they want you. We can significantly negotiate up every single one of the fees and contracts on the table here. One door might be closing, but a floodgate's bursting open! Say the word and I can set up a few weeks of lunches and meetings with every single prospect on this table. I can handle it, Hope. All you need to do is say yes. I could be very good for you. I understand you. All that psych-profiling, all this time watching your life, reading what you think and feel about it."

Rachel's long, thin fingers dance across the papers, "Everything here plays to your unique ability to engage with other people and infect them with your joie-de-vivre. There's plenty to keep you occupied for a year or two at least! What you're looking at on this table is probably your first three million dollars." Pleased with herself, she teases, "You'll finally be able to pay Everett back for those fancy boots he bought you."

My glazing eyes scan. Occasionally, a recognisable logo leaps out and my heart jumps. Rachel's pretending nonchalance, but when I glance up, she's watching me intently.

"If the show's over, does that mean my marriage has to be?"

"No, Hope. A proper officiant married you. It's all legal. The show is neither here nor there. You're Everett's wife. He's your husband. You can't change that unless you get a divorce."

The knowledge Rachel isn't here to separate us is an inexpressible relief, but… "Why did you choose to come today?"

Rachel's immediately on the defensive, "What difference does it make? I had a window in my schedule!"

Undeterred, I persist, "But you've known about all this for *many* days, yes?"

"A few…"

"So why come now, when you were fully aware Everett wouldn't be here? It's almost like you *planned* it."

She sighs, "I had to be ready! Everything on this table is an active offer, Hope, and I know that because I've spent the last week checking out every single one of them."

"Why not speak to both of us at the same time? Everett will need to know the show's over…and why shouldn't he know about all of this?"

"…Because these decisions aren't Everett's to make. They're yours."

"It's all a bit of shock."

"Of course it is…and it'll be a shock to Everett, too. That's why you need time to get your own thoughts in order before you explain things to him. I can tell you now, he ain't gonna like it."

Apprehension grips me again, "Why not?"

"Because I'm proposing a little time away from home…and I'm not talking a couple of days."

"What *are* you talking?"

"A few weeks…?"

"How *many* weeks?"

"Come to New York, have a taster of what's on offer, listen to some pitches, make some pilots, get a feel for what it could be *like*. Don't tell me it doesn't secretly get you even a *little* excited?"

"It gets me a lot excited, but…"

"But? You could be on tv, like Oprah! Now, you empower bored, unfulfilled women to rediscover the magic in their day-to-day lives. It's nominative determinism, Hope! You're a walking, talking bubble of optimism! Imagine how much more effective that message could be on your own show or with your own regular column! How about a number one bestseller about Ridge River with your name all over the cover? Personally, I would *love* to do all this stuff, but people just don't like me the way they like you – "

"Rachel, that's not true – "

"They don't, Hope. Your charm makes you so marketable, and you don't even realise! Please, *please* don't throw this chance away. Can you honestly sit there and tell me you won't regret it if you refuse to come?"

She pauses, reaches for a cookie from the plate on the tray, demolishes it with urgent bites like a pecking sparrow.

"Say something, Hope! Anything! Just give me a hint…"

"I need to think, Rachel."

"I guess you don't have to decide *right* now – "

"I can't decide right now! I need *time* – "

"Time's the one thing we don't have much of. I can give you a couple of days and then people are going to need firm answers, one way or another."

"Can I keep all this stuff and read through it?"

"Sure. Keep the paperwork, read it tonight. Sleep on it. Call me the day after and give me your decision. No more pressure. I've made my pitch. I have your best interests at heart as well as my own. Fifteen percent of a shitload of money is…a shitload of money! The more successful *you* are, the better I'm doing. As far as I'm concerned, this is a team effort. Your desperation brought you to my door. My show gave you the second chance you needed. Now's the time to fly, Hope."

HOPE

"This is another level, Hope!"

"I know…and the best thing about it is they're coming next week to take all the cameras away. It's perfect timing! Not only have we got all the new customers my promotion's brought in, but there's still time to get the old clients back too. It's the best of both worlds for the hotel!"

"But that's not what we're here to talk about, is it?" Mel observes, shrewdly.

"I don't know what to do."

"Are you *crazy*? I can't believe there's a moment's hesitation in your mind!"

"What about Everett?"

"Oh, good Lord, he's a big boy, Hope. He'll cope. The one thing Everett knows how to do is sacrifice. He will be sad if that's what it takes to guarantee your happiness. You know that."

"*He's* the reason I can do all this! He gave me the self-confidence to try. Nineteen years of my first marriage and I didn't accomplish a single thing. Less than six months of my second marriage and I'm setting the world alight, Mel, or so it seems! That's not just coincidence, is it?"

"Honey, everything happens for a reason. Every decision you make leads you somewhere, but *you* still have to make the most of the journey."

"That's easy for you to say, you're a success! You're good at everything, you're confident, you've got it all worked out – "

"You just see what I want you to see. You don't actually know a damn thing about what I am. I'll tell you what I'm good at, Hope – the only skill

I've ever possessed. I'm world-class at digging in and not letting go. Maybe *I* should have been the bullrider, huh?"

"I don't understand."

"There was no guarantee that I would end up here, with my hundred-dollar hairstyle and my five-star hotel. That isn't where I'm from at all. My parents were well-meaning, God-fearing, hard-up, bland people, Hope. My Dad worked in the tyre factory like half the town, and my Mom stayed home, cooked, cleaned, and drank vodka at ten in the morning when she thought no one would know. She was unfulfilled, bored and bitter."

"Fucking hell, she sounds like me! How old were you when you got with Jesse, then?"

"I was seventeen…and nineteen when we married."

"Blimey! I thought I was young getting married at twenty-one!"

"I didn't get married because I wanted to be someone's wife. It was just a way to get out of town. I was never intending to get married at *all*! I got married because I swiftly realised becoming Mrs Jefferson Cole Jnr was the cleverest thing I'd ever do!"

"Why?"

"In my senior year I got with this boy called Dirk."

"Dirk? Seriously? Is that a name?"

"Uh-huh…and Dirk was a total dick! He played football. He looked like Roger Ramjet. He was a shit to me, but all my friends told me I was lucky to have been selected by Dirk and I should shut up and put out. I lost my virginity to Dirk the asshole, got treated like total crap by him, and just kinda thought that was how life was for girls like me."

"Did you *know* Jesse then?"

"Yeah. Jefferson Cole was this little runt with a stutter so bad he could hardly talk. As far as I was concerned, Jefferson Jnr was less than nothing to a princess like me. I don't think I'd ever said a single word to him in my life!"

"You absolute bitch!"

"Damn right."

"So, what happened to make the scales fall from your eyes?"

"My Dad had this buddy called Nick. They'd been friends since they were kids, and Nick was married to a lady called Kimberley. Kim loved riding, and had a horse called Pearl who was her prized possession. Kim got breast cancer, and she died from it…and Nick was so heartbroken he couldn't bear caring for her horse every day. He asked my Dad to take it away and find a new home for it. So, in the paddock behind our house, we ended up with this horse we didn't know what to do with. My aunt told my Mom I should learn to ride, because it's not every day you get given a horse for free."

"Fair point."

"While she was up visiting, we all went to the local rodeo for an evening out, and who should be competing but Jesse Cole! I was expecting to see him fall flat on his nerdy little butt, but he was *amazing*! He aced the night, won everything he entered in his age group, and swaggered out of there laughing and joking with all the other guys like he totally belonged, *and* with a roll of cash in his pocket. The mystery of how he could afford such a nice truck was suddenly solved! My Mom obviously clocked him too, because his truck was pulling up outside our house the very next Saturday morning. She'd organised for Jesse Cole to come around and teach me how to ride Pearl the horse. I was mortified! What if someone found out that Jesse Cole the tongue-tied dweeb had been at my house by invitation?"

"Melanie, you aren't doing yourself any favours here!"

"Oh, I was horrible, Hope. I don't mind admitting it."

"What happened? Did you have your lesson?"

"I had to! My Mom and Dad were there watching, and Uncle Nick came over, so I couldn't act up because of him. It would have been sorta disrespectful to Auntie Kim's memory to refuse to ride her horse.

Jesse was so calm, and Pearl just stood there and did as she was told. I don't think Jesse looked directly at me once for the whole two hours he was there, but he explained things real patiently. He could see I was scared, so he held the bridle and got me walking around. Mom and Dad looked pleased, and Uncle Nick was smiling, and I felt as if I was doing something good for once. Then it came time to get off the horse, and I made a bit of a hash of it – "

"Yeah, my first dismount wasn't too graceful either, I seem to remember."

"I pretty much fell off the side of her, and Jesse caught me. I remember being so shocked! Compared to Dirk, he was skinny, but he was so *strong*! In every way, he wasn't what I expected. He let go of me and stared at the toes of his boots and pretended nothing had happened. My Mom and Dad came over, and Uncle Nick, and they were crowding around, all excited about how well I'd done. By the time I looked again, Jesse had gone. It was only later that evening I realised he hadn't stuttered once."

"What happened after that?"

"My Dad paid him to come over across the summer to teach me to ride. He'd come faithfully on a Saturday morning and we'd tack up Pearl together, and he'd get me to practice different things with her. I started to realise what a nice, straightforward person he was. You always knew where you were with Jesse. We were gearing up to graduation. My Mom was putting pressure on me about getting a job. Where? Doing what? I had no idea. I wasn't any good at anything. Jesse and I used to sit in the long grass under the trees once my lesson was over, drink a soda and laugh our heads off. With Jesse, I just felt free of everyone else's expectations…and then one day he rode over on his rusty old pushbike, and I asked him where his fancy truck had gone. He said he'd sold it to pay towards an RV. I asked what the RV was for, and he dropped the bombshell that his Dad had agreed to finance him to try his luck on the circuit. In a matter of weeks, he was off on the road all on his own to make a go of his dream. He'd been saving his winnings and working towards his grand plan all through high school. He so impressed me then! He was driven and mature. He knew what he wanted and he was going for it. I just grabbed the front of his shirt in both my hands and went, 'Take me with you!'"

"Mel, I love this! It's like a film!"

"Hardly. In a movie, it would have been happily-ever-after then and there."

"But it wasn't?"

"No! Jesse just said, 'Don't be crazy, Mel. You'll hate it.' I remember he was still holding my hands where he'd taken them off the front of his shirt. I blurted out all this stuff about how my Mom drank secretly because she hated her life, and how if I couldn't get away I'd end up just the same as her, probably married to Dirk, and how horrible he was, that he treated me like a piece of meat, and that if Jesse let me go with him, I could help out by doing the laundry or something. I started to cry and he just stared at me in total shock…and then eventually he very grudgingly agreed I could tag along, if I promised not to be high-maintenance."

"So, he wasn't desperate for you to fall for him?"

"No way! He was going to be a rodeo star, and nothing was getting in the way of that, least of all whiney little Melanie Masters from down the street."

"That's so funny!"

"I have always needed Jesse much more than he's ever needed me. My mother told me repeatedly not to marry a poor man, and I made sure I didn't."

"I'm loving this!"

"I went home and informed her that in a matter of weeks I'd be leaving with Jesse Cole, and she said over her dead body was I going to live in an RV with a boy when I was barely eighteen years old. I did some quick thinking and said we were engaged, which changed everything! Then, my mother was delighted, and only too happy to pack me off into the unknown with someone they hardly knew. I had to shoot over to Jesse's fast as I could, before word got out, and explain we needed to pretend to be engaged so I could leave town with him. Luckily, he just thought it was funny."

"This is so cute. Then what happened?"

We went on the road and it was hard, hot, boring…but Jesse was great company, and we got used to one another and the little routine of our life. We laughed an awful lo, and talked endlessly about our hopes and dreams, and one night we just ended up making love, and it was great. Jesse was a virgin and didn't know what to do, and my only experience of sex was lying underneath Dirk the meathead, so I guess it was pretty fumbly, but my memory of it is that it was sweet, and gentle, and it felt like the most natural thing in the world to be with him.

A little while after that, he won some decent money, bought me a ring, and said if I wanted we could be engaged for real. A few months later, we got married. He had his first championship in the bag before he was twenty-one, and we've never looked back. Everything I have is because of Jesse."

"You've looked after him for nearly forty years, Mel. He needs you too."

"Sure, he does *now*. I've been around so long I'm a part of the furniture – but at first he didn't want or need me at all. He thought I'd just slow him down. I dug in, Hope. Like you, I saw a chance and I went for it, and I made it work for me. I made myself indispensable to Jesse and now, like you say, he can't do without me.

What I'm trying to say is you took the chance on coming here, and you've worked to create this wonderful opportunity for yourself. You *have* to take it! Trust me, Hope, Everett will understand. I know it in my heart."

EVERETT

Hope wriggles, uncharacteristically restless. Gruffly, I grunt with mock severity, "Goddam it, woman, will you stop fidgeting?" tickling her so she can't help but wriggle more.

She sniggers, elbowing me in the ribs, "Get off!"

Chuckling, I hug her more tightly and she relaxes back against me, sighing softly. We lie cosy and quiet together in the centre of the big bed, listening to the February gale howling outside, the occasional spattering of ice driven forcefully into the windowpanes on the harsh winter wind.

"Are you gonna tell me what's eating you or do I have to torture it out of you?"

A sharp intake of breath, then the exhalation of resignation. She has to talk to me because I've given her no alternative.

"You left, and the whole world convulsed!"

"Because I went to a farm show?"

"No…that bit was coincidental."

"Good, because there will be times in the future when I have to go away to stuff…"

"Right… And maybe I will too."

"Huh?" Did I just hear her right?

Hope turns over, wraps her arms around my neck and presses her soft cheek to mine, whispering, "Look at the camera."

Silky strands of her hair have fallen across my face. I stroke them aside and peer across the dark room at where the camera should be. No red light winks back at me as it normally would, "There's no light."

"No."

"Oh, Hope, you haven't broken the camera, have you? You'll get roasted by Producer Rachel if you have."

"No, it's not that."

"There's no light!"

"But it's not broken."

"How do you know that?"

"Because I had a long conversation with Rachel yesterday, and she told me the network have pulled the plug on the show. It's over!"

"You're kidding? Why did they stop it?"

"Because Sylvie left Regis, and Bill has been having a secret affair with someone in the production team! Seems the whole thing collapsed like a house of cards."

I roar with laugher, "Priceless! Hey, it wasn't that little Japanese girl he used to flirt with non-stop was it?"

"Was she called Tamika?"

"Don't ask me to remember names! Whoever she was, he had the hots for her. What happened with the others?"

"She packed up and left him."

"Poor Regis. He was a nice kid."

"Wasn't he a Mountie or something?"

"Not every Canadian is a Mountie, Hope."

"No, but I'm sure he was – "

"He was a Ranger of some kind, don't ask me what. So, that's it. No more cameras, no more stupid rules, no more screwing under the covers fainting from heat exhaustion…"

"Is that all you're worried about?"

"No…but it's a bonus."

"Someone is coming next week to remove them all, forever!"

"Hallelujah! I won't miss those suckers one little bit."

"Me neither. There won't be any money coming, though."

"Jesus, Hope, I don't give a shit about the money! I didn't sign up for that. I got what I wanted."

Hope's soft lips brush my cheek, "Darling…"

"Why were you so edgy about telling me? It's great news!"

She combs her little fingers rhythmically through my hair and I bask in the sensual pleasure of being home.

"Because that's not the only thing Rachel came to tell me."

"Hold on…what? She *came* here?"

"Yes. Yesterday…and she brought a camera crew with her. I thought that was a bit like overkill until she told me our cameras were off. I couldn't believe I hadn't noticed…"

Apprehension tightens my stomach. Rachel Delany is a busy, influential woman. She wouldn't bother catching a plane from East coast to Wild West in the worst depths of winter without a very good reason.

"She came all the way out here with a camera crew?"

"Yes." I can hear the tightness in Hope's voice, and feel the tension in her body.

"Why?"

"It's more good news…but…but…"

"But?"

"It's going to change some stuff in our lives, I think."

"Will you start making sense, please?"

"Oh, just put the light on, Ev. I need to show you something."

She slides away from me and leaves a block of unwelcome, cold air in her place. I shiver, reaching for the bedside light. I can already hear Hope opening the closet door, the rustle of paper. We both squint at one another in the sudden brightness. She gets back into bed next to me, pulling a large canvas shopping bag with her. Her eyes are very wide in her thin, white face. Her habitually smiling mouth is a hard, flat line. I swallow, try to keep it light, "What's in your bag, baby?"

Wordlessly, she extracts item after item, piling them across our laps. They're heavy on my thighs.

"What *is* all this?" I pick up papers at random, glancing over them, putting them down. My cursory appraisal is sufficient to acquaint me: contracts, offers of employment, project proposals, requests for appearances and personal interviews. Hope's bright eyes haven't left my face. Meekly, she ventures, "I think it's my future."

I try to smile at her but I can't get it right. I catch sight of myself in the dressing mirror across the room. What's on my face is less a grin than a grimace, utterly failing to mask my pain. She strokes my chest, "You're angry, aren't you?"

I smile again, and this time at least it looks like one; weak, melancholy, but recognisable all the same, "Of course I'm not angry."

"But you don't think this is good news?"

"I do, honey. I truly do. Good news for you, but bad news for me."

The sides of her mouth pull down as if she might cry, and she pushes her lips so tightly together they turn white with the pressure.

"Hey…" I put my arms around her, nuzzling my face into her neck, "I told you this would happen, didn't I? I knew I couldn't compete. Little ol' me versus all this amazing potential? But that doesn't mean this isn't good news. It doesn't mean it isn't a wonderful opportunity for you…and Rachel brought all this with her yesterday?"

"Yes."

"Wow. The world wants you, Hope," I kiss her bare shoulder, "Get out there and meet it!"

"Really?"

"Hope, look at this stuff! Interviews, magazines, newspapers, tv! What's this, a publisher? Is this a book deal?"

She nods, "There's a couple in there."

I shake my head in wonder, "I'm so proud of you. Look at what you've done! Opportunities like this don't come knocking twice."

She nods slowly, fingers spread out like stars across the pages on our laps.

"I assume to do this stuff you have to go away?"

More nodding.

"Where?"

"New York."

She reaches up a hand to clasp my arm, "It's not too bad. Rachel says eight weeks and I'll be back."

I snort sarcastically, releasing her from my embrace to grab again at the piles of contracts, "That's crap, Hope! She only said that so you'd agree to go. Look, this is filming a tv pilot. There's something about recording a series of radio shows in here as well," I shuffle through everything, trying to find it, "How long do you think just those two things will take? And then there's all the other stuff…and I presume you'll need some time to eat and sleep as well, or is Rachel proposing you give those a miss for two months?"

"Don't be facetious, Everett!"

"Well, don't be naïve, Hope! There's some seriously meaty shit here. You ain't gonna be no eight weeks, and Rachel knows it. She just plucked a figure out of the air that didn't sound too daunting, to make you go along with her plan."

"Don't you trust Rachel?"

"No, I don't! I'm not suggesting she's a crook, but she *is* a businesswoman. What's she getting out of this?"

"Fifteen percent of everything she negotiates for me."

"Okay, when you get to New York, get a lawyer, *independent* of Rachel. Get advice, and get a proper contract drawn up between you – none of this verbal crap!"

"You really don't like her, do you?"

"Rachel ain't doing this 'cos she's your buddy, Hope. She's doing it because she can see you're destined for greatness. She wants a little of your gloss to rub off on her. If you decide she isn't a good agent, you fire her and get somebody else."

"I wish *you* could be my agent."

"What do I know about all of this?"

"But I feel protected from harm with you around."

"Honey, I'm still gonna be here. I'm not going anywhere. If you need me, all you do is pick up the 'phone, get on a plane, come home. Whatever happens, you will always have a place here."

"You talk as if I'm going away forever!"

I hold her close to me so she can't see the expression on my face, and tickle her again until she squeals and wriggles, the papers sliding and spilling haphazardly from the covers to the floor. As she winds her luscious, warm body around mine and I savour the sight, sound, scent and softness of her, I can already feel the chill of lonely nights nipping at my uncovered heels. Whatever Hope might believe, I understand the reality of this. I can predict what will happen. In my head and in my heart, I already know the magic's over.

When she leaves for New York a week later, I drive her to the airport as I promised I would. She kisses me goodbye with undiminished passion, and reiterates, "Eight weeks and I'm back, okay?" but she's fizzing with dangerous excitement, like a lit firework. Every ounce of strength I possess commands my reluctant arms to release her from my embrace, to set her free.

She waves, blows kisses and all-but-runs through the gate into Departures as if she can't wait to be gone. As I always knew they would, eight weeks turn to ten, twelve, sixteen…and I begin to die inside.

****

At first she calls me every evening, bubbling with what's happened during the day, words tumbling over one another in her haste to tell me everything.

It doesn't take long before relaxed, chatty evening calls become texts in snatched moments, and then another message, another meeting, another delay, another excuse.

I'm not surprised, but that in itself is sad. I knew this would happen. Once I began to understand what Hope was capable of, I knew I wouldn't be able to keep her. I was touched by her earnest assurances that nothing would change. Everything that's being thrown at her and she expects to return in a matter of weeks unaltered by her experiences? I suppose that's the attraction of Hope. For my beautiful wife, no matter how bad it gets, tomorrow is always another day where something truly wonderful might happen, if you wish hard enough.

HOPE

I'll be somewhere – in a taxi on my way to a dinner meeting, or travelling to an interview – and I'll be staring across the endless lines of crawling traffic, observing the press of buildings encroaching from every side and blotting out the sky, and I'll find myself wishing to see our view, the afternoon sun glinting blindingly off the river, making the pink-tinged mountains glow. I'll realise I haven't rung Everett like I said I would, and fall to fretting over whether it was yesterday I called him, or the day before, or perhaps there's foundation in my sudden anxiety that I haven't called him this week at all...

I allow indignation to swirl with the guilt. It dilutes it. He hasn't rung me either! But perhaps he doesn't want to bother me because he knows I'm busy, that there's a lot to pack into my crowded days, that Rachel's 'phone doesn't stop ringing. It's ringing now in fact, from her bag between us on the taxi seat, and then I'm earwigging because it's about me, and the intention to ring Everett is forgotten again. By the time her call is over, we're at our destination and my attention is demanded upon matters other than husband and home. Another day disappears in a haze of bewildering busyness. I can't telephone a man who rises at five when it's already two in the morning and I've only just got back to my hotel suite. Tomorrow, without fail. I'll call him tomorrow.

EVERETT

I read the magazines she's featured in, and the articles she writes. I love what she does and how she does it. I tell everyone.

My favourite is her internet radio show. She has great guests, terrific on-air allure, a marvellous gift for comic timing, a superb line in the disarmingly-insightful question, and the content's always thought-provoking.

I look at pictures of my scruffy, carefree, spirited little wife primped, preened and styled, and barely recognise the dazzling stranger whose hypnotic eyes burn from glossy covers. I find myself staring at the close-up images, convinced at any moment she'll blink. She seems so vivid, and yet unreachable.

Once in a while, she'll call. She still sounds inspired and enthusiastic, but increasingly weary. I'm worried about her. I try to gently suggest a little break, but there are voices in the background, her attention being demanded, no time for irrelevancies like health and home when there's money to be made. She hurries me off the 'phone, promising to call later. She never does. Even though I know it's not intended as a slight, it still feels like one. She's not coming back and I must come to terms with that, learn to weather this pain as I have the others in my life, tamp it down and cover it with the thick mulch of work and responsibility, so that in time it'll rot away.

HOPE

Sleeping's a problem. Although I'm occupied and excited during the day and exhausted by the evening, night time is when the vulnerability ambushes me, when I begin to question my ability to deliver everything being demanded of me.

I want Everett. I miss him. These are the times I want to call him, but I can't. It's the middle of the night. He needs to sleep. If the choices I've made are messing with the comfort of my routine, that's not Everett's fault, and he shouldn't have to suffer by having the pattern of his own days disrupted by it.

I start by lumping the heavy duvet, trying to cuddle up to it as if it's a comforting body in the bed beside me. It doesn't work. I try a line of pillows, but they squidge flat as I roll onto them. The bolster provides the best solution. Solid, heavy, thick and firm, over six feet in length, when turned vertically down the bed and tucked in beside me it's a serviceable Everett-substitute, a decoy for my troubled longings, something to press myself against in the impersonal, empty darkness of the hotel room.

The bolster helps me settle more quickly to fitful sleep, but it's not right. None of this is right. It's the roar of traffic on the wet streets storeys below my high-rise window, rather than the gush of the waterfall into the rocky ravine. There's hooting of horns and shouting of voices, rather than the rustle of wind in the trees, the whinnying of the horses or the lowing of the cows. The smells are unpleasant: drains, food, dirt and pollution, instead of the crisp scent of the pines, the rich aroma of the meadow grasses, even the sharp tang of manure wafted on the wind. The sights fail to impress. Buildings and monuments are no match for forest, river, trail and mountain. Despite the months I've now spent here, New York is not home and it never will be. I have only one home and it's in Wyoming. It's open, wild, unpolluted and peaceful, and my wonderful husband is there.

How can I transplant the success I'm enjoying here to the serenity of home? It's impossible, isn't it? To exploit the opportunities, I must be where they're generated. It's got to be one or the other. To go home is to give up, to fail before I've reached my personal pinnacle, and I'm not ready to do that yet. I know I have more to accomplish, but to remain here indefinitely is to slowly perish without what succours and sustains me: Everett's nurturing love and the nourishment of Ridge River. Is it any wonder I cannot rest?

THE BOYS

Everett's before the whiteboard, frowning, rubbing things out with a grubby cloth, scrawling amendments with the squeaky nib of his marker pen. Suddenly, he tuts, mutters, "Shit, I forgot…" glancing around and catching sight of Walker, who's snuggled around Rosemary on the sofa, impatiently waiting for her to finish writing up her notes so they might have the early night he's planning...

"Walker," Everett beckons him. Walker reluctantly uncurls himself from Rosemary and eases wearily to his feet, padding across the room, "Boss?"

"Do me a favour, buddy. Go down and shut the gates. I forgot to do it earlier...and have a quick walk around and make sure everything's okay. I need to stay here and get my head around this."

Without considering it might be a foolish thing to do, irritated that his pleasurable plans are being disrupted, Walker snaps, "Come on, Boss, can't somebody else go? I was looking forward to an early night, know what I mean?"

Walker jerks his head across the room towards Rosemary, still deep in her textbook, and misses the dark cloud that passes across his employer's face. Icily, Everett replies, "I asked *you*, Walker."

Walker rolls his eyes like a sullen teenager, sighs vocally, turns to grudgingly comply with the instruction, muttering not quite under his breath, "Just 'cos *you* ain't getting any..."

Before he knows what's happening, Walker's head is nearly wrenched off by the Boss getting a good hold of his collar and yanking him backwards, gripping the front of his shirt in both fists and throwing him hard against the wall with one big hand around his throat, roaring, "What the fuck did you say?"

Walker, airway severely constricted, can only gasp, gurgle and stare in bug-eyed terror.

Nathan and Hedge drop the Xbox controllers and scrabble to their feet, ongoing digital rivalry instantly forgotten. Rosemary's cry of horror wakes Bobby from his doze on the other end of the sofa. He splutters and hauls himself upright, "What's goin' on?"

Tim races down the corridor from his room, alerted by the commotion, rushing up to Everett and placing a gentle hand cautiously on the older man's shoulder, "Boss, take it easy. You're strangling him!"

Everett ignores him, snarls, squeezes harder.

"Boss, what are you doing?"

From behind them comes Rosemary's impassioned plea, "You're hurting him! *Please!*"

That brings the Boss to his senses. His head snaps around, his wide eyes stare at Rosemary as if he's never seen her before, then he gasps, drops Walker as if he's ablaze, staggers backwards and thumps down on the end of one of the benches, slumping forward with his head in his hands.

The only sounds are the irritating racket of the computer game soundtrack and Walker hacking for breath. Rosemary rushes over and throws her arms protectively around her boyfriend. Bobby snaps off the Xbox and propels the youngsters out of the kitchen. They're too amazed to protest, gawking over Bobby's massive shoulder as he drives them down the hall before him like calves out to pasture.

Everett scrapes visibly-shaking hands through his hair, "I'm so sorry, Walker... I never meant... I don't know what came over me."

Walker swallows, winces at the discomfort, croaks, "Forget about it. Guess I'll go shut those gates..."

Rosemary clings to his arm, "I'll help you."

Tim looks from Walker's pale face to Everett's bowed head.

The Boss stares at the tiles between his feet and shudders like a man in shock.

In the yard, Rosemary tugs Walker underneath the outside light and examines his already-bruising neck.

Tim pulls the door firmly shut and demands with quiet authority, "What the hell happened in there?"

Walker scowls, trying to bat away Rosemary's caressing hands, "I'm all right! I opened my stupid mouth, man, that's all."

Tim rolls his eyes, "What's new? What did you say to deserve that reaction?"

"He told me to go shut the gates and do a night check 'cos he was dicking around with the rota. I whinged, 'cos I had something *better* do to, you know?" Walker grins, and draws Rosemary towards him with a casual arm about her neck, bending to nibble her earlobe. Rosemary giggles, and Tim snaps in a furious whisper, "Walker!"

"Keep your panties on, Princess! I merely suggested that just because *he* wasn't getting any, he shouldn't take it out on the rest of us…and he lost his *mind*!"

"Are you surprised? You're such an idiot sometimes!"

Walker rounds aggressively, hissing harshly, "Hey, it's not my fault she's left him!"

Rosemary interrupts, anxious to defend Hope, "She hasn't left him."

"Oh no? I thought she was only supposed to be gone two months, and what's it been…four, five?"

"She's *busy*! Have you seen all the stuff she's doing?"

"Yeah, all the fun she's having, all the money she's making… That's why he's being such an asshole twenty-four-seven. He knows she's having a better life somewhere else and there's nothin' he can do about it."

Tim shoves Walker's shoulder, incensed at his lack of empathy, "*You're* the asshole! He *misses* her! You know when Rosemary goes to visit her folks and you're a complete prick to the whole world until she comes back again? He's hurting! It's the same thing!"

"Is it? I'm not so sure 'bout that. Rosemary goes for a few days, she calls me while she's away, and I know when she's flying back because I go to the airport to fetch her. Seems Mommy stopped calling a while ago…and as for when she's coming home…?"

Rosemary attempts to diffuse the mounting tension, easing in between them, placing her little hands on Walker's chest, pointing out, "Well, she's kind of a celebrity now."

Walker's index finger jabs the air triumphantly, "*Exactly*, baby! What's the poor old Boss got that can compete with that?"

Tim shakes his head regretfully, "Walker, that's harsh. They're good together. You know it."

"Maybe…but they ain't together now, are they? She's away living the high life, and he's left behind taking it out on us!" He rubs at his tender neck with one rough palm, prophesying, "Trust me, Timmy, she ain't *never* coming back, and he knows it."

HOPE

I wake with the bleeping of my 'phone alarm. It takes me two attempts to turn it off. My fingers don't feel connected to my hands, which in turn seem loose on the ends of my arms, which themselves appear as if they're coming adrift from the rest of me.

I roll onto my back and bump the bolster. A moment of elation before I realise and give it a spiteful jab with my elbow, as if it's the bolster's fault it's not my husband. Flopped against it like a discarded ragdoll, I stare blankly across the room at the open bathroom door. I've got to get over there. I need to shower, get ready. Today is the day I perk myself up. I've been like this since *Christmas*, lazy and sluggish. I need a kick up the arse. As there's no one else here to administer it, I'm going to have to give it to myself. No more luxuriously-decadent room service breakfasts. No more taxis on expenses. I can't use the cold weather as an excuse any more. I can no longer claim I don't know how to get around. It's been four months, plenty of time to explore and settle. I'm going to *walk* the few blocks to the studio today, and I shall purchase myself a healthy breakfast on the way.

It's an effort to lever my unwilling body out of bed, first rolling to hands and knees, then reversing ponderously out from under the covers like a sow emerging from a wallow. Dizziness hits me as I straighten up. The room whirls, my eyes refuse to focus, the throbbing sensation like persistent period pain gripes my stomach as it's been doing for the past couple of days. I stagger to the bathroom and clamber inelegantly over the high rim of the roll-top tub, standing before the taps and jerking the stubborn mixer to shower setting.

I stand under the variable water flow, sometimes a gush, more often a trickle, unpredictably scalding one moment and lukewarm the next. I stare down critically at my vastly bulging stomach. I feel bloated and unhealthy. I'm becoming plumper than I was before my divorce. I've much preferred being slim, athletic, strong. My clothes look better. I feel fitter, healthier, livelier, and I was proud of being a middle-aged woman in great shape, until I arrived here and it all went to pot. I know Everett admired my figure, and he's in terrific condition for his age. It's up to me to reverse this decline. He won't say anything, but I know he'll be disappointed if I return home a fat, blousey frump from six months in the city. Much as I'm appreciating all that's happening to me here, I know this lifestyle is bad for my long-term health. At Ridge River, eating well and being active was easy. There was nothing better to do than go outside, surrendering to the irresistible compulsion to explore the beauty and wonder of every inch of the place. New York's so different, and not in a good way. My life is lived in hotels, taxis, boardrooms, bars, studios and recording suites. These days, I only walk from the table to the sideboard for another complimentary Danish, from the bar to the toilet at a celebrity soirée, or in distracted circles around my hotel room like a caged tiger, desperately fighting the panic of a looming deadline and a lack of inspiration.

Ashamed, I smack my palms onto my wet buttocks and wobble them vigorously. Not as dire a situation as the protruding vastness of my stomach, but certainly chubbier than they've been for a year or two. Weeks of gluttonous weight gain do mean my bee-sting boobs are reasonably magnificent for a change, but on balance I'd rather wave goodbye to them to recapture the overall trim, toned body of last year.

I wince and rub my lower stomach with both hands as another period pain contracts my muscles. I can't understand why I've been having a few days of cramps and only spots of blood. I cast my mind back to last month, but things have been so hectic I struggle to remember.

Suddenly I'm desperate to urinate. Irritably, I snap off the shower and climb unsteadily out of the bath, wrapping myself in a towel and sitting on the toilet. I pee powerfully and for a considerable time. I'm relieved to see a quantity of blood on the toilet paper. At last, something normal is happening! Another sharp spasm takes my breath away as I stand. Wow, it's *bad* this month, probably because I'm not eating properly or keeping fit.

As I towel my hair dry, I hunch over to relax my muscles and ease the mounting severity of the cramping. I could do with an hour on the sofa instead of having to high-tail it across town to record a talk show, but I chose this. I can't let a bit of period pain get in the way! Look at the discomfort Everett puts up with every day and never complains. He does what needs to be done no matter how much his shoulder plagues him. I need to take a leaf out of my tough husband's book and get a bit braver.

I shuffle awkwardly to the bedroom to dress, attempting to exert mind over matter. The sharpness of the pain brings me up short as I bend to select underwear from a drawer. A couple of deep breaths and it lessens. I glance at the bedroom clock. I need to get a move on! I dress hurriedly and refuse to notice how poorly I'm starting to feel. A healthy breakfast and a brisk walk in the sunshine will sort me out.

****

Reaching up to the highest shelf, the griping pain that's been steadily increasing in intensity the further I waddle up the block from hotel to studio suddenly jabs me more brutally than it has since waking, as if one of Everett's powerful horses has flicked up a hoof and driven it without warning into my lower stomach. I gasp aloud, snatch back my reaching arm and double over, fingertips pressing the shelf in front of me as giddy nausea strikes. A passing man seems to think I'm defeated because I can't reach, grinning expansively, picking the brioche off the shelf and placing them jauntily into my basket. With typical British pluck, I instantly pretend to be quite well, levering myself upright by supreme effort of will, managing to tinkle a gay little laugh as he tips his baseball cap charmingly and slopes off, pristine trainers squeaking on the shop floor.

The agony abates somewhat, but still I hold my breath, every muscle tensed to withstand a fresh stab. Looking left and right, I'm relieved my section of aisle is now deserted. I lower my basket to the floor with deliberate care and cautiously tilt my tender body forwards to grip the shelf directly in front of me with both hands, exhaling a whistling breath. Slow and steady seems to be the key here; no violent movements to antagonise the pain monster and set it frantically gouging at my insides once more. I'm sweating profusely. My blouse is sticking to my back. My temples itch with the trickling beads of moisture in my hair, like a million insects crawling against my scalp. Something bad's going to happen any minute, and it doesn't feel like period pain any more. I must have something gastric. Hardly surprising I've caught a germ in the sweltering, stinking heat of the filthy summer city, especially given how drained I've been these last few weeks. However, the idea I might soil myself in a grocery store I frequent almost daily is too embarrassing to contemplate. I need to leave my basket, get home before I have a humiliating accident, place myself within dashing distance of the loo, call Rachel and tell her I'm too ill to do the recording today. I know it's letting her down, but right now all I care about is how utterly dreadful I feel, and how alarming it is.

I've got to go home, *now*. I've half a block to stagger and the pain is building unbearably, mushrooming into a threatening, pressing mass low down in my stomach. I know I must run, but I can't move. Trying to take a single step, even attempting to slide my shoes across the linoleum, produces pain the like of which I have never experienced, cleaving vertically through my vagina, slicing my lower stomach like a ripping blade and shooting straight to my chest, snatching my shallow breath and leaving me heaving for oxygen in the airless aisle, unable to do anything but grip the shelf before me in my tightening, whitening fists.

To my horror, I become aware of an uncomfortably wet sensation spreading outward from my groin and down my thighs. My thin trouser fabric sticks to my legs. Almost too far gone with incising agony to understand what's happening, I glance down at the crotch of my slacks with a surprising degree of detachment, expecting to be hit at any moment by extreme mortification, dread and distaste, only to be stunned by the sight of dark blood seeping thickly through the linen, forming fat, heavy droplets on the outer surface of the material, elongating in glutinous trails that swing to splatter the floor between my spread feet.

There's a dreadful noise, a high-pitched screeching it takes me several seconds to realise is coming from my own mouth. Two women in grocery-store tabards are running up the aisle towards me from the direction of the cash registers. Another scimitar stroke of pure pain and my shuddering legs buckle. The first woman reaches me and grips me around the waist, holding me up. I just have time to grasp her arm and groan an apology about the state of the floor before blackness descends like the heavy drop of a final curtain.

****

The drip in the back of my hand pulls tightly and makes me feel queasy as I reach across the bedside table for my 'phone. I rest back against the pillows and close my eyes. I feel bruised, exhausted, wrung out by the utter confusion and extreme emotion of the past forty-eight hours. This is the first rest I've been able to snatch. I focus with difficulty on the 'phone screen, scrolling through my rapidly-expanding list of contacts to find the correct number, steeling myself for the reception I'll get when the call connects, hoping I have sufficient battery-life remaining to properly explain myself.

"Hope? Where *were* you! I've been calling and calling! You dumped me right in the crap! I had to piece together a show in ten minutes from your notes!"

"Rachel...I'm sorry...I – "

"Sorry? Is that the best you can do? That might wash in Wyoming, Hope, but here in New York we *deliver* on our commitments!"

Tears prickle my eyes and a tight sensation grips my throat. I whisper, "Rachel, *please*..."

A note of unease tiptoes around the unforgiving edges of the Brooklyn twang, "Hope, are you okay?"

My voice slurs and fades with tiredness. I made this call and now I don't have the energy to explain, "I'm sorry I didn't ring. Something happened... I couldn't."

"Hope, you're freaking me out! What's going on?"

I take a deep breath. I've thought about this for hours. It's the right thing to do. It squares this crazy circle of life I've drawn, but I'm not sure

I've got the will to go through with it, "Can you get down to the Presbyterian?"

I shift in the bed and wince with a jolt of instant discomfort, as Rachel squawks, full-volume, "You're in *HOSPITAL*? What's happened? An accident? You jaywalk like crazy – "

"It's okay, there's not been an accident…"

"Are you sick? You're sick, aren't you? I said you were looking pale, didn't I? Didn't I say that?"

A nurse appears at the bedroom door with a wheelchair. It's time again. I feel an immediate surge of strength and purpose, "Just shut up and listen a minute, will you? Do you want the reality tv scoop of the century?"

"Huh?"

"*Do* you? Do you want to stick it to all those stupid old men who pulled your precious show?"

Unsure where this is going, Rachel nevertheless can't help herself, "What do *you* think?"

"Right. Forget everything we've already got in the diary, cobble yourself together a camera crew and get your arse downtown. Something's happened here that might just make your month."

EVERETT

It's Friday, so when I hear a car draw up outside I assume it's a visitor for one of the boys, the latest chick they've gotten their spurs into so deep she's prepared to drive all the way up here at this time of night. I don't think anything else of it, but settle back down to my book, trying to remember where I've got to. As I read down the page to find my place, I realise I haven't taken any of it in…or the page before…or the page before that… I'm not concentrating on anything but my growing dread. The second week in a row a stand-in presenter has covered Hope's radio show, with no explanation beyond the briefest mention of her 'taking a little break for personal reasons'. Well, I'm her husband and I have no idea what those reasons are. I've tried calling. Her cell goes straight to voicemail without even connecting. I leave messages. She doesn't call back. I try Rachel. I can't get through. The line is permanently engaged. I even try ringing the number for the 'First Sight' production office, but now the show's cancelled that team doesn't exist. An operator reconnects my call. I get Vasquez's voicemail. I'm annoyed at what I'm convinced is deliberate evasion, impotently furious I can't discover what's going on with my own wife no matter how many answer machines I shout at.

I tell myself she's a grown-up and she makes the choice to get in touch. But two weeks, not even one call home, an absence from her beloved show without explanation, and some serious avoidance from everyone who might know what's going on? It's crossed my mind to start calling the hospitals, maybe even the cops to report Hope as a missing person…but what's stopping me is the fear she isn't missing at all. What if she's made a decision about the course of the rest of her life? Perhaps she's moved on in more ways than one? If you met somebody new, it sure would cramp your style to have your rejected husband calling your cell every ten minutes unable to take a hint.

Tears rush into my eyes. I squeeze them shut. I'm not going to cry about it. I fidget in the chair, sniff loudly, flick irritably back to the start of the chapter. As I've not absorbed a single word I've read this evening, I might as well start from where I left off yesterday.

Insistent rapping on the French doors makes me start. I sigh, discarding my book on the footstool. Clearly, our nocturnal visitor has never visited before, and can't locate the correct door. Boy, is she going to get a shock when it's the boss who lets her in! I absently ponder which one she might be here for. The smart money's on Mo, who plays the field with the sort of carefree abandon I once attempted myself.

I get up, wincing as my shoulder twinges. There's no one to massage ointment into it any more. I shuffle wearily across the room. The heady scent of the pines assails me as I swing open the door to admit the myriad beguiling perfumes of midsummer dusk.

Instead of the anticipated teen in tight denim, a blinding light shines directly into my watery eyes, making me squint and blink, disorientated. Recovering, I discern the all-too-familiar silhouette of sound guy with microphone boom, and a camera man edging forward for the inevitable close-up. Behind them both, I recognise the gawky outline of Rachel, juggling ubiquitous clipboard and cellphone, attempting as ever to both write and text at the same time, as if there's never enough hours in the day to accommodate her boundless ambition.

Instantly convinced this has something to do with my increasingly-frantic voicemail messages, my terror renders me immediately defensive. I'm suddenly certain I'd rather not receive Rachel's explanation, particularly if it confirms my worst fears about Hope leaving me for good. I recall the last time Rachel paid a visit. In my opinion, her unwelcome reappearance augurs only negative news for me. I take a breath to launch into a tirade about the cheek of their unannounced arrival, about to suggest they'd better get their skinny butts the hell off my property, when I notice another figure standing nervously to one side. All the wind instantly leaves my sails and I'm adrift. Staring, gasping, mouth dry, throat clicking, I'm unable to make a sound. The presence of Rachel and her camera team is utterly forgotten.

My usually-glowing wife looks worryingly ill. She seems pale and exhausted, with dark rings under dull eyes, swaying slightly as if she's almost too weak to stand. Her normally-lustrous hair is lank and unkempt. Her pallid cheeks flush as her anxious eyes meet my unconcealed dismay. I see she's clutching something against her chest, but can't make out what it is in the dark. Tentatively, she whispers, "I'm sorry. I should have called, but it got to the point where I'd broken so many promises about ringing you that I was afraid to – I didn't know what sort of reception I'd get – but it would be two in the morning, I'd be longing to call, and I couldn't. I couldn't knowingly disturb you just to satisfy me. Our lives got out of sync somehow. I let the connection between us break and I didn't know how to get it back. My fault...*all* my fault..."

I want to tell her it isn't, that *I* could have called *her* – but I was too busy feeling sorry for myself to swallow my goddam pride and pick up the 'phone. I could've hauled my selfish butt onto a plane to New York and surprised her...but I didn't do that either. I sat here, brooded, festered, shrivelled, soured.

"You know when we went camping up above the waterfall that time, and we saw that shooting star? You said I should wish on it, remember?"

I nod, dumbfounded, as she takes a couple of cautious steps forward into the circle of light, turns the pink bundle towards me, and I realise what it is she's clasping so protectively.

"I never said anything to you 'cos it seemed a bit daft...but I *did* wish, Everett...and it came *true*..."

I know I should reach out to her, but I can't move. I can only stare...

"I've missed you so much. I haven't been able to sleep because you weren't there. I was living half a life because you were missing from it. I know I had to go and do what I did...but now I'm petrified it wasn't worth it. Has spending too long away from you ruined everything we had?"

I manage to gurgle, "You should have *called* me. *Someone* should have *called*..."

"I wasn't avoiding you! My 'phone battery was dead! I've only just been able to charge it and hear the messages you left. Every other part of life had to wait until the immediate danger was past...and it is, so the doctors say. I've been day and night in the premature baby unit. I've barely slept, I've hardly eaten. I've just been watching and hoping and *wishing*...

We've been through a terrible time this last couple of weeks, but we'd both really like to come home now – if that's all right with you."

I'm incapable of coherent speech. I know if I open my mouth all I'll be able to do is howl at the moon. Explanations can wait. Nothing else matters but that Hope has come back to me. I take two quick steps out into the cool night air, fold my wife and tiny daughter into my arms, hold them close, and feel resurrected.

www.ingramcontent.com/pod-product-compliance
Lightning Source LLC
Chambersburg PA
CBHW020647260626
47157CB00008B/2947